Unwrapping Christmas

Also by Lori Copeland

Morning Shade Mystery Series
A Case of Bad Taste
A Case of Crooked Letters
A Case of Nosy Neighbors
Child of Grace
Christmas Vows

Brides of the West Series
Faith
June
Hope
Glory
Ruth
Patience
Roses Will Bloom Again

Men of the Saddle Series
The Peacemaker
The Drifter
The Maverick
The Plainsman

Stand-Alone Titles
Monday Morning Faith
Simple Gifts

LORI
COPELAND

Unwrapping Christmas

ZONDERVAN®

ZONDERVAN.com/
AUTHORTRACKER
follow your favorite authors

ZONDERVAN®

DEC 0 5 2007

Unwrapping Christmas
Copyright © 2007 by Copeland, Inc.

Requests for information should be addressed to:
Zondervan, *Grand Rapids, Michigan 49530*

Library of Congress Cataloging-in-Publication Data

Copeland, Lori.
      Unwrapping Christmas / Lori Copeland.
         p. cm.
      ISBN-10: 0-310-27226-2
      ISBN-13: 978-0-310-27226-7
      1. Christmas stories. 2. Domestic fiction. I. Title.
PS3553.O6336U59 2007
813'.54—dc22

2007012725

This edition printed on acid-free paper.

Interior design by Melissa Elenbaas

Printed in the United States of America

---

07 08 09 10 11 12 13 • 10 9 8 7 6 5 4 3 2 1

To my special family, the ones who love, support, and encourage me. I couldn't make it without you. Lance, Randy, Rick, Russ, Gage, James, Joe, Josh, Audrey, Maureen, Shelley, and Grandma Opal. I love you guys. Thanks for putting up with all my busyness.

advent

Advent

Advent is the beginning of the church year for most churches in the Western tradition. It begins on the fourth Sunday before Christmas Day, which is the Sunday nearest November 30, and ends on Christmas Eve (December 24).

"Advent?"

Rose turned an eye to her refrigerator where her already overburdened calendar hung. Rank smells wafted from the brimming trash can that her husband Joey had forgotten to empty. "What about it?"

"It's for the bulletin. Pastor wants little bits of information on Advent's origin, traditions, how long the season lasts. Then it might be fun to throw in how other countries observe the Christmas holiday." As the ace secretary at Bethlehem Messiah Church, Kay put the merriest slant on the request, and Rose knew by the time she hung up, her calendar would have another starred check mark. The beginnings of a migraine gripped her temples.

Rose eyed the overflowing sink stacked with breakfast dishes. Her two teenagers could open a cabinet, select a bowl and spoon, find the milk in the refrigerator, heap sugar on frosted cereal, and eat. But somehow they were rendered helpless on a full stomach to rinse their dishes.

Instead, they'd dump them into the sink with the glowing assurance that mom would come along and locate the dishwasher.

Kay's voice jerked her back to reality. "Think you could do that for us?"

"I guess I could." *I guess I could*, Rose's inner voice mimicked her standard mantra. "How soon do you need the information?"

The fall church craft sales were over, and the crocheted toilet-paper roll covers and wooden rearview cutouts of a woman bending over in the garden were put away for another year. Folks had already flocked up north for their annual pilgrimage to see the leaves, so gorgeous along the North Shore. Performances for Christmas pageants, orchestra, choir, and theater goings-on would soon be in high gear, along with outdoor reenactments by amateurs and professionals.

"As soon as possible. Pastor Ralph wants something cheerful to kick-start the holidays."

"Sure. I'll see what I can find."

Next month St. Paul would host the Winter Carnival with its masterful ice and snow carvings, a treat Rose and the family never missed, and one that took them away from their home in Nokomis at least a couple of weekends during the month. Better to get her good deeds in early this year so she'd have a viable excuse to refuse later on.

"Thanks, Rose. We knew we could count on you!"

Rose punched the "off" button on the phone. Facts about Advent season. The request wasn't difficult, just time consuming, and time was a precious commodity. She whipped the kitchen into order and emptied the smelly trash. A batch of brownies went into the oven for her teenage son Eric's youth meeting that night. Turning to the huge box of Christmas decorations her husband Joey had lugged from the attic last night, Rose scanned the years of accumulated seasonal knickknacks: holiday wreaths that had seen better days, two ceramic cookie jars, a snowman, and a slightly cracked laughing Santa face that Anna had dropped when she was three.

Carefully peeling back the tissue from the family Advent calendar, Rose thought of all the years this timely tradition had given the family. It wouldn't be Christmas without the calendar. A treasured family heirloom from the Black Forest, beautifully carved, the calendar was formed by tiny cubicles where a small nativity figure nestled behind the date. Grandpa Karlsen had purchased the keepsake for Grandma Louise in Frankfurt, Germany, while serving in the army during World War I. Family legend had it that she scolded him severely for spending money on something that wasn't a necessity. It had been passed down to Rose's mother, and in turn she had passed it on to her daughters who shared custody of the priceless heirloom. This year the calendar would grace Rose's home.

She set the Advent calendar on its special shelf above the table in the sunny kitchen nook and located the first piece, then put the tiny hand-painted cradle at the foot of the date of December 1. She stood back to admire her work.

Warm sunshine filtered through the bare branches on the sugar maple tree standing just outside. Minnesotans gave thanks for a mild early winter day like this one.

Rose focused on the brown lawn. Joey had been so busy, he had neglected to winterize the birdbath. The round concrete bowl needed to be turned over so it wouldn't collect water and freeze. Like every holiday season, Joey put in long hours at South Side Transport, the family trucking company. Business was always brisk around the holiday season.

Joey wasn't the only one chasing his tail—they'd all been busy. Christmas meant church activities added to an already hectic schedule. Rose felt the familiar tightening in her stomach, the painful pierce of "how will I do it all?" starting to creep through her psyche. Christmas should be more than frantic activities, hectic crowds, and overworked husbands. The holiday held deeper significance and Rose knew it—it wasn't that she didn't want to slow down, but life got in the way.

This year she would go through the motions for the sake of her family, but that inward elation, the joy she once felt, was missing. Truth was, she was just too tired from putting up all of the decorations, hanging lights around the roof, and baking endless cookies. She was so busy *doing* Christmas, there wasn't time to *experience* Christmas.

She shifted the calendar, tilting it just so. The movement jostled December 1, and the wooden square tumbled, struck the white kitchen table, then rolled behind a chair leg. Dropping to her hands and knees, she squeezed through the chair support bars, her hand groping for the piece.

Her cell phone tinkled an animated version of "Jingle Bells," a ring tone her fifteen-year-old daughter, Anna, had chosen for the season.

Rose's head shot up and smacked the hard bottom of the table. Tears welled in her eyes. *That'll sure help my headache.* Frantically rubbing the smarting area, she backed out of a maze of table and chair legs. The stench of burning brownies reached her nose.

"Jingle bells, jingle bells, jingle all the way!"

She spent precious seconds frantically searching for her oven mitt. Smoke started to roll from the sides of the oven door. The smoke alarm went off, and above the pulsing shriek, the cell phone played its tune.

"Jingle Bells, jingle bells, jingle all the way!"

Rose located the mitt, shoved it onto her right hand, opened the oven door, and yanked out the pan of smoldering brownies. Then she dunked the smoking pan in the sink and reached for the phone with her left hand. A plume of steam fogged the shadow box window.

Snatching up the phone, Rose caught the last notes — "all the way!"

"Hello!"

"Rose?" Sharon Walker chirped.

"Yes?"

"Did I catch you at a bad time?"

Rose fixed on the smoke and steam spewing up from the sink and was able to fan the air in front of the smoke alarm to silence its shrill cry. Her fingers explored the knot on her head, not surprised to find it the size of a cheese cube. "Did you need something, Sharon?" Sharon was the Sunday school social director.

"Lois Gleeson had emergency gall bladder surgery this morning."

Rose sobered. "I'm sorry. Is she okay?"

"She's doing nicely; she can come home in the morning. I'm arranging take-in meals for the coming week. Can I put you down to help on Friday and Monday evening? She'll need something with fiber, no dairy content, and low fat."

As much as Rose wanted to voice a refusal, she couldn't. But where would *she* find time to prepare additional food and deliver it two evenings this week? She'd have to crowd it in between basketball and choir practices, but how could she refuse Lois? Lois had carried in meals for her family when Rose was stricken with the flu last winter.

"Sure, I'd love to help!" She closed her eyes, head throbbing, and reached for a pen to scribble the dates on her calendar. Without the trusty calendar and day planner she carried in her purse, she'd forget to dress some mornings.

They chatted a few minutes before Sharon excused herself to make the remainder of her culinary mercy calls.

A loud clatter shattered the silence after they hung up. Rose slowly turned to stare at the calendar shelf, now hanging lopsided, secured to the wall by one bracket. December 1 was probably somewhere between the kitchen and the next block.

Rose collapsed in a chair, a mental to-do list racing through her mind. Church, the Christmas program, thrift shop, brownies, fix dish for Lois, and on and on. And on. How could she possibly get it all done? And what would Joey say about her taking on even more? Lately he had seemed a little irritated at her constant running and doing, but wasn't she doing the Lord's work? How could she say no to any one of the requests? She'd promised God to do everything her hands found to do, and to do it well.

Suddenly she felt every ounce of her thirty-eight years crowding her.

advent

ENGLAND
Merry Christmas

The custom of sending Christmas
cards originated in England, a nation rich in varied traditions. Window candles attract carolers, who
fill the air with Christmas music.
A Yule log finds its place of tradition in the hearths of some homes in
England and Wales. Children hang
stockings by the chimney or their
beds, hoping Father Christmas will
bring them gifts. Christmas feasting
includes the wassail bowl and flam-
ing plum pudding. On Boxing Day,
December 26, gift boxes and alms
are distributed to the needy.

Rose slid into the church pew, glanced at her watch, and sighed. She'd made it. Pastor Ralph was starting services, but instead of preparing her mind for a blessing, all she could think about was how she had somehow survived the last hour. Joey's office meeting had run late, Eric's basketball practice went longer than usual, and Anna's cheerleading clinic had gone into extended session. Nobody had eaten. There wasn't time to make dinner since she had to stop by the local grocery to replace the burned brownies she was obligated to provide for Eric's youth group. She mentally assessed her near-empty pantry for dinner choices. She'd whip up a batch of tuna salad even though they'd already eaten fish three times this week. Her family might grow gills, but at least they'd have their omega-3 requirements met for the month.

She slid further down in the pew and relaxed. She was alone, not an unfamiliar state. Joey hadn't made it home in time for services, but the kids were in their respective youth groups. Because of meetings and separate class activities, the family rarely sat together these days. She kept an ear tuned to the pastor, but her mind was on the church-affiliated thrift store. Thursday was her morning to work. Seasonal clothes were pouring in, and they all had to be sorted and tagged.

Business was brisk and she had a feeling some of the people were doing their Christmas shopping by choosing good quality items that showed little wear. It made her heart ache to think some people had to buy used clothing for their children's Christmas, particularly when she considered the bounty her own children would receive. She was indeed blessed. That was why she tried never to resent the time she spent volunteering at the thrift shop.

She released a mental sigh, checking her watch again. She was exhausted and her head ached. She hoped Pastor Ralph didn't run over tonight, because in addition to dinner, she had to plan a casserole to take to Lois on Friday night. Something with fiber, no dairy, low fat. Checking to make sure no one was watching, she eased her day planner out of her purse, her eyes scanning the crowded pages. Why did she have such a hard time saying no? For one thing, after a couple of sermons on how Christians were expected to bear fruit, she felt guilty if she even thought of refusing to help.

She could have easily drifted off or passed out, and either would have been a welcome relief at that moment.

Gradually she became aware that something had changed. People were listening more intently. The pastor was through, but people were still sitting. The room grew quiet as someone walked to the pulpit. Rose blinked, trying to focus. It was time for the service to be over, yet a member of her Sunday school class was speaking. It was Jean Farris, and tears streamed down her cheeks. Cold chills ran up Rose's spine. Jean could barely speak as emotions rattled her thin body. She and Jean had been friends for years, babysat for each others' kids. What could be wrong ... ?

"... I need your prayers and support. Today, my husband's chest X-rays came back questionable. Of course they're running further tests — we have to wait and see ... "

A hush fell over the congregation. Rose shifted in the pew, her heart going out to the anxious wife. She thought about Jean and Ken's two children — a boy, twelve years old, and a girl, eleven. Jean homeschooled the kids and had no other job; how would she manage if anything happened to Ken? How would Jean cope without Ken's steady influence? Without her loving husband?

Wait. She was borrowing trouble. The tests could come back negative, or the X-rays could have been faulty ... that was possible.

Worrying a damp handkerchief in her hands, Jean poured out her heart. "I don't know what to do, where to turn. If anything happens to Ken ... " She sank to the front pew, her shoulders shaking from barely suppressed sobs.

Ken Farris, robust, the picture of health, a deacon who was highly respected for his moral values. Rose shook her head in disbelief. How could he be this ill and she not know? Although Jean said his X-rays had come back ... what? Questionable? Jean hadn't mentioned a word about him feeling ill ... or had she? The past month had been a blur with the start of basketball season and the church craft bazaar.

Jean continued from her seat. "I've never faced anything of this magnitude. I need—" She sobbed openly— "help. Someone please help us."

Silence followed. It was the sort of loud stillness that made you want to do or say something, but Rose knew she couldn't trust her thoughts or her words. Ken could be facing a critical or even a terminal illness. The implication was so overwhelming, Rose couldn't compute.

Pastor Ralph immediately lifted the concern in prayer—petitioning God for strength and healing. Rose prayed silently for peace and comfort for Jean and Ken. A wave of compassion filled her. *Please, God, give them strength to bear this ordeal.* She put herself in Jean's place. If this were Joey ... She shoved the thought away, unable to bear it. Joey was her life.

Prayer requests continued, but all subsequent problems faced by neighbors, aunts, and cousins paled in comparison to Jean's crisis. Rose's eyes moved to the freshly hung garlands and festive tree, and tears welled in her eyes. She quickly dashed them away, blocking emotion. Her friend sat in the front pew, alone and miserable, lost in anguish.

Jean remained in the pew when the service ended. Relief filled Rose when she saw a few members begin to gather around. She knew she should say something, needed to say something, but what?

Her heart ached for her friend. She glanced at her watch. The kids would be waiting in the car. Hungry. Cranky.

Stepping to the front row, Rose waited for an opening and then quickly enveloped Jean in a supportive hug.

"Oh, Rose ... How could we go on without him?" Jean murmured.

"Everything will be fine," Rose soothed, but her mind ranted other thoughts. *Why don't I say what this is? Horrible. Ghastly! Without Ken, Jean's life — her two children's lives — would be turned upside down. Say something more concrete! Tell her that what she's facing is serious and there are no words to express your distress. Confess that you don't know what to say, but you desperately want to help. Tell her that you don't have the power to change the situation, but God does. Say something other than a banal, "Everything will be fine."*

Rose knew Jean had to be questioning why God would allow something so potentially terrible to happen to this wonderful man and his family. Rose didn't have an answer—she only had her faith. At this hour, fear had stripped Jean of that precious element. Ken and Jean served the Lord, they raised their children in his ways. Why did God permit illness? Death? Rose searched for words that would bring comfort to this troubled and confused wife, but she came up empty. Platitudes failed in the face of real crisis.

Rose lifted her voice above the din. "Please don't hesitate to call me if you need anything. Meanwhile, try to be positive. Maybe it's just a blip on the X-ray." She squeezed her friend's shoulder supportively. Leaning closer, she whispered, "I'll pray for you."

Feeling she had failed Jean, Rose straightened and smiled at Mrs. Johansson as the older lady pushed in to say something. Rose realized she was actually grateful for the reprieve. For the first time in a long time, she was thankful to leave. She checked her watch: 8:15.

She still had to make tuna salad for supper.

Joey was waiting when she walked in the door. She felt a rush of gratitude as she looked at his dear, familiar face.

Thank God he was healthy, but then no one had suspected Ken was ill. Life was uncertain; it was wrong to waste one minute of it.

"Hey, honey." He hooked an arm around her neck and kissed her. "What's for dinner?"

"Tuna." She kissed him back.

"Again?"

"Starving kids in — "

"I know. Be thankful for what we have."

She added another kiss. "Dinner will be served in fifteen minutes."

She mixed the tuna while Anna filled glasses with ice and poured soft drinks. Rose should have stopped for milk on the way home, but she was just too tired.

The family gathered around the table. Anna seemed preoccupied tonight, smiling occasionally, as if she knew a secret. Rose made a mental note to ask why the grin? But later. Tomorrow was a school day and both kids had homework.

When dinner was over, she and Joey lingered at the table talking. She told him about Ken.

He shook his head. "Man, I hate to hear that. Ken's a good guy."

Rose sighed. "It could be nothing, but I felt so helpless, not knowing what to say. Do you think I'm insensitive?"

Joey met her worried gaze. "Where did that come from? You're the most sensitive person I know. You just don't always notice things."

She grimaced. "Like what?"

"Eric didn't have much to say tonight. That's unusual for him."

Rose dismissed Joey's observation. "He was just tired. He's a growing boy. Anna was grinning like a Cheshire cat, but that doesn't mean anything either."

"I think it's more than that with Eric. With me working so much overtime, he's alone too much."

Rose sensed the unspoken criticism behind his words, and she prickled. She did *not* ignore her children or their needs. "I'm here."

"No, you're not. Most of the time you're off volunteering somewhere, or at the church."

"Are you saying that's wrong? I'm serving the Lord." And where was Joey coming from with all this censure? Eric had his own agenda, and he knew she and Joey were there if he needed anything.

His eyes caught and held hers. "Are you really? Or are you just busy?"

She threw her napkin on the table. "I can't believe this. You're saying I shouldn't work in my church and my community?"

"The Bible says we're to be moderate in all things. It's good to help others, but not at the expense of your own family."

He pushed back from the table and walked out of the room, leaving her to stare after him.

Well ... how dare he?

Seemed Scrooge had arrived early this year.

3

The church-affiliated Second Time Around thrift shop sat at the top of a small grade. The road curved up the hill with a sharp turn at the top, leading into the paved drive. Rose maneuvered the U-turn and eased her van into the parking lot. She'd been up since dawn, working on the bulletin fact sheet. The job would be a breeze, and it was informative to learn more about Advent and its true meaning. The congregation would appreciate her efforts.

This morning the sun had all the warmth of a candle flame, but it was sunshine, and she appreciated it. Slipping the key into the lock, she opened the shop and stepped inside, pausing to glance with silent pride at the racks of clothing with sizes and prices precisely marked. Someone had left a couple of black trash bags sitting by the front door. People weren't supposed to leave donations when the store was unattended, but she had a feeling the person who left the sacks didn't want to be noticed. Most folks made nice contributions, knowing they would be resold to county residents who couldn't afford to buy new, while others found the shop a convenient disposal for annual closet cleaning. The winter season brought an influx of new business.

Rose dragged the overstuffed bags inside and went to hang up her coat in the volunteer break room. She put a fresh pot of coffee on and went back to open the trash bags. A light pink polyester blouse looked fairly nice. She held it up in front of her, inspecting for flaws. No spots, no visible tears—and then her jaw dropped so low she could have stepped on it.

No buttons. Every button had been neatly cut off, leaving short stubby threads that stuck up like orphaned tufts.

She dropped the blouse, reached in the sack, and pulled out a blue jacket. Again she held a garment in good condition. Size ten. They had a lot of requests for jackets like this one.

But no buttons.

She could not believe this. Surely it was a fluke. She upended the bag, dumped the contents out on the counter, and pawed through the items. A flowered skirt that looked vaguely familiar. No buttons. A white blouse with a touch of embroidery on the collar. No buttons. Did Nokomis have a button thief in town? What kind of Scrooge donated clothing to a thrift shop and cut off the buttons? Did they think the customers were flashers? Someone should put up a sign stating the thrift store was not the town dump.

A dark green suede jacket caught her eye, and in an instant she knew the identity of the button clipper. There were only two jackets like this in town—one of them hung in her closet at home. The other belonged to Jade Patterson.

Blonde, blue-eyed, tall, thin. Attorney's wife, Jade. A social trendsetter who'd rather be caught without makeup than be seen out in public wearing a garment identical to someone else.

Rose sighed. She loved Jade, but she could be a bit dramatic at times. Both had worn their jackets to services one Sunday, and they sat on the same side of the auditorium. At first, Rose had tried to pretend that she hadn't noticed she was infringing on Jade's fashion, but with practically every woman in the congregation switching their eyes back and forth between the two, that strategy went down the drain in a hurry. The coincidence was a minor thing, not exactly a world-shaking event when you considered the daily news. She'd smiled when someone pointed out the fashion faux pas, but evidently Jade had been compelled strongly enough to donate a perfectly adorable jacket to the thrift store and cut off all the buttons. *Why?*

Rose folded the clothing, putting the items aside for the time being. Maybe someone would donate buttons.

She tossed the blouse onto the counter, glancing up when the door opened and her coworker, Blyth Samuels, entered. Blyth was always well groomed and tastefully dressed. But today she looked like a fire sale. Her orange and blue flowered blouse clashed with a fuchsia skirt. Rose's gaze traveled to the woman's feet. Flip-flops. In Minnesota in early December? This wasn't like Blyth. Her expression was blank, as if she wasn't aware of her surroundings.

"Hi!" Rose said.

"Yes, hello." Blyth wandered past, heading toward the back room. She looked neither to the left nor right. Her rubber soles flapped against the concrete floor.

Rose stared after her, curious. Blyth had never been particularly chatty, never inclined to gossip or comment on items brought in, but she usually paused to pass the time of day. Was she ill?

Her coworker disposed of her coat and wandered past again, hollow-eyed and passive. Rose shoved a box aside and decided to investigate, but Blyth was so distant, it took a moment to find an opening to broach her bizarre behavior.

"Can you believe this?" Rose showed her the blouse. "Why would Jade strip buttons off her donations?"

Blyth shrugged. "People are odd."

Yes, they were, and Blyth was certainly doing her share to perpetuate the behavior. Rose kept a close eye on her and noticed she was going through her usual routine with careless mistakes. Judging by the vacant look she occasionally cast around the room, it was easy to see she had something on her mind.

Rose priced and hung new contributions while keeping her worried eye on the other woman. Her behavior was almost frightening, but obviously she didn't want to talk about whatever was disturbing her.

Finally she'd had enough. Around noon Blyth spread her brown bag fare on the red Formica-topped table in the break room. Rose decided she should stay longer today. Obviously Blyth wasn't herself. "Are you okay?" she asked the other woman.

Blyth looked up. "I guess so, why?"

"You seem distracted."

"Distracted?" Her smile didn't quite surface. "No, I'm not distracted." She picked up her fork and mechanically started eating.

Rose eyed Blyth's green salad and wished she'd brought something. Though she barely would have had time to whip up more tuna salad before she'd run out the door that morning. What happened to the days when the kids were smaller and she'd plan and prepare balanced meals?

Blyth mechanically chewed, but Rose realized the woman could be eating cardboard for all she knew. She took a bite, stared into space, and took another bite.

Stared. After minutes of robotic movements, Rose sighed and reached over to take the fork from Blyth's right hand. "I have a soft shoulder, and you're more than welcome to lean on it."

Sudden tears formed and rolled down her coworker's cheeks. She didn't look like she was crying. Her face didn't get all red and crumply the way most people's faces did. She just sat there with rivers of tears streaming from her eyes.

Concerned, Rose bent forward. "I won't bite. I promise."

Blyth shook her head no and Rose swallowed her relief, hoping Blyth hadn't noticed. Whatever it was, she wanted to help, but she just wasn't sure she could. Her shift was over, and she really needed to leave. So much to do ... Yet Blyth looked so tortured.

Her heart skipped a beat when Blyth's mouth opened and the dam broke. "It's my son, Frank. He's using drugs."

Drugs. Every parent's nightmare. Her Eric was a good kid. He'd never given them a moment's trouble, so she didn't know what to say. First Jean, now Blyth. Was God testing her compassion this holiday season? She had compassion, but she had never found adequate ways to express it. Yesterday, Rose thought if she took a cake to an ailing friend, she was ministering. Today, two women needed

more than flour and sugar; they needed the oil of under-
standing, and she was completely out of her comfort zone
as she sat there feeling helpless.

She cared, of course she cared. But what more could
she do?

Platitudes raced through her mind as she searched for
the most comforting responses. *God is always near. Everything will be fine. Just pray about it.* None of them held water.
Blyth's son was a druggie. Words couldn't erase the horror.

"Frank doesn't come home until the wee hours of the
morning. I pace the floor, waiting for him to come in,
praying. I'm so afraid he won't come, terrified the police
will arrive and tell me he's been in a terrible accident, or
worse, that he's overdosed." Blyth fished in her pocket for
a clean tissue.

"I'm so sorry," Rose whispered. This woman's son's life
hung in the balance, and all she could think to say was
"I'm sorry"?

Only God could change the situation. Rose wasn't
God. Blyth was a member of her church, but in a different
Sunday school class, and the church was large. They only
knew each other through volunteer work. Blyth needed
someone she knew and trusted to console her, to help her
through this tragic time.

Rose awkwardly patted the other woman's hand,
sneaking another quick glance at her watch. Her shift was

over, and customers were already gathering at the checkout counter. "Is there anyone you can talk to? Pastor Ralph— perhaps a fellow Sunday school class member?"

Blyth looked up. "I'm sorry. I know this isn't your problem."

"Oh no, I *want* to help. Do you have a good study Bible? I can provide one, and you're welcome to talk to me anytime. I mean it … "

Blyth lifted a silencing hand. "Frank was a good kid until he got involved with the wrong group. He's a joiner. He wants so much to be accepted by his peers. My husband died last year, and it's just the two of us. I pray for him with every breath, but it's easy to feel God has forsaken us."

Rose sobered. "God never forsakes us." She was on solid ground now. The bell over the door chimed. She glanced to the front of the store, relief and guilt filling her when she realized the intensely private conversation was over. They couldn't talk and wait on customers at the same time. "I'm sorry. Customers."

Nodding, Blyth wiped her eyes on the tissue and pushed back from the table. "Thanks, Rose. Unless you've had the problem, you can't possibly know how good it is just to talk to someone."

Reaching for her coat, Rose wondered why she wasn't feeling all warm and fuzzy inside, confident that God had put her here to minister to a sister in a time of need.

She was here. Blyth surely had a God-sized problem. She had offered a study Bible, a good study Bible that could address many of the worried mother's concerns. She made a mental note to drop the Bible off at Blyth's house even if she hadn't requested it. She was only scheduled to work a half day, but she couldn't leave Blyth alone and upset. She couldn't. She laid the coat aside and waited on a customer.

Twenty minutes before quitting time, Rose cornered Blyth in the back room. Blyth's words had lingered with her, haunted her. "Blyth, I know I haven't been through what you're experiencing, but I can pray for you."

Blyth offered a weak smile. "Right now?"

"Well . . . yes." Actually, Rose had thought more along the lines of each praying in her own private element. But now that Blyth had mistaken her offer for immediacy, she guessed they could pray right now. Her mind churned with all she had yet to accomplish today—dinner, choir practice tonight, laundry. She had always been uncomfortable praying out loud. Maybe Blyth would take the initiative, and she could squeeze her hand in support.

Blyth bowed her head and waited.

Rose bowed her head. "Please—feel free to start if you'd like."

"I'm so emotional, can you?"

"Sure." Clearing her throat, Rose grasped both of Blyth's hands in hers. "Lord." Her mind searched for the poetic—

beautiful, comforting, profound petitions uttered to offer peace. She even heard an echo of David, the mighty king of Israel's anguished cry, "O my son Absalom! My son, my son Absalom!" For a moment, she experienced a faint revelation of what Blyth must be going through. If this were Eric, she'd be on her knees, begging for grace, but in search of the eloquent, her mind went blank. What came out was anything but profound, it was lame. "Lord, we ask that you take care of Blyth's son. Thank you for our blessings and this lovely weather. Bless this holiday season and ... Amen."

"Amen," Blyth softly echoed.

Well, she might as well have asked God to throw in a box of buttons for all that prayer accomplished. Yet she was sure he knew the words when the burden was too much, and the Holy Spirit uttered the petition for her.

All things considered, neither people nor problems had changed that much since King David's time. An anguished prayer for a wayward child. A parent's vulnerability. Hopefully what Rose felt and couldn't verbally express, Blyth sensed.

They lifted their heads and let go of each other's hands. Blyth wore a naked expression, like she wanted to linger and talk, just talk, but she got up to wait on an older woman. Rose got her coat and purse.

"Everything will be fine," she told Blyth at the door. She leaned forward and awkwardly hugged her.

"Thanks, Rose. I'm so thankful you stayed through the afternoon. I know you're busy."

"Never too busy to help a friend." Her eyes softened. "Call me anytime, Blyth. I don't have the answer, but I can always listen."

Rose walked slowly to her van, hefting the bag of buttonless clothing. She had decided that even if she was weak in ministerial skills, she was confident with a needle and thread. She would store the bag in the hall closet to work on later, knowing she would be hard-pressed to get to choir practice on time. Practice was every Thursday until the church cantata, scheduled for the eighteenth. And then there was the Advent church bulletin project—that needed attention too.

Something about Blyth's lost expression lingered with Rose. Had she helped? Or had she merely slapped a Band-Aid on a torn artery? She pushed the thought aside. Everyone was rushed these days. Blyth understood.

Rose whispered a quick prayer of thanksgiving that Eric wasn't on drugs. A faint glow of self-righteousness raised its head, and she promptly squelched it. She wasn't a better parent than Blyth. God didn't love her more. She had no idea why Frank had chosen drugs and Eric had not, but she was grateful. She said a prayer for Jean and Blyth, making a mental reminder to call Jean for lunch this next week. She didn't want to put that off for too long.

So much trouble everywhere she looked — children rebelling, illness, despair. What must God think of the chaos?

At least she and Joey were on solid ground. Maybe their relationship was not as exciting as the marriage manuals advocated, but it was solid. They didn't spend a lot of time together, with him working day and night and her involvement in the church and community.

But Joey was a rock. A hard worker, a deacon in the church.

Trouble had barely touched her family; she prayed life would stay that way.

4 chapter

Dinner. If Rose could talk her family into one less meal a day, life would be simpler. She reached for the phone to call in an early pizza order. Everyone liked pizza. They wouldn't mind having it again tonight. Better than tuna. Food ordered, she threw a load of clothes in the wash. With the second load sorted and piled on the floor, ready to go, she checked phone messages. Just the usual stuff. Patsy Baker, two houses down, wanted her to watch their place over the holidays while she was away. She'd already agreed to do that. Patsy couldn't remember up from down, but she was a good ole soul.

Celeste Horner had called to say that the weekly Bible study would be at eight-thirty, instead of nine in the morning. Thirty minutes wouldn't wreck Rose's schedule, but the time change meant she'd have to get up earlier if she wanted to stop by the post office first.

The front door opened and slammed shut. Ah yes, one of their resident teenagers had arrived home. It must be close to four. Footsteps headed her way. Rose waited. Anna appeared in the kitchen doorway. "I'm home."

"So I hear. How are you?"

Enter the no-spin zone. Depending on how her daughter's day had gone, they were either in for a short period of mother-daughter bonding or an explosion that would rupture gas lines all over Minnesota.

Anna, tall and blonde like her Scandinavian ancestors, with eyes the blue of a placid lake, slumped in a chair. "What's for dinner?"

"Pizza."

"Again?"

"Okay, you can have tuna."

"Mom!"

"Pizza or tuna. Your choice."

"I like pizza; I just don't like it *four* times a week. Why can't we ever have meatloaf? And mashed potatoes. Or pot roast, like Sara's mother cooks."

"There are starving children that would appreciate pizza … "

"Mom." Anna gave her an exasperated look.

The washer shut off and Rose disappeared into the utility room to load the dryer and put in a second load. They were either the dirtiest or the cleanest family on the block—she couldn't decide. Wet towels and stained gym socks built up faster than she could tackle them. Back in a few minutes, she picked up the conversation. "I'm sorry. I'll fix a real meal next week. Maybe spaghetti?"

"Spaghetti's a real meal?" Anna slumped. Apparently something was on her mind other than her dinner entrée. "Nick Chalmers asked me to the church New Year's Eve Watch party. Can I go with him?"

Rose's internal alarm sounded. The Chalmers boy was three years older than Anna and had a truck so jazzed up it sounded like a Canaveral rocket. Her precious baby, in the same vehicle with that boy? On New Year's Eve?

"Mom, it's positively awesome that he even noticed me!" Anna sat up, apparently revived. "He's so cute!"

Yeah, Rose could remember a few of those "cute" boys from her teen years, and she didn't want her daughter going out with Nick, a senior in high school. "What happened to Dale?" Sharon Walker's son. Good family, honor student from what she'd heard. Anna's age, fifteen.

"He's taking Cindy." Anna got up from the table. "Can I go?"

"No, the Chalmers boy is three years older than you." She wouldn't further inflame her daughter by mentioning the truck, but Anna wasn't getting in a rocket.

"Mom!"

"No."

"That is so unfair."

"Anna, I'd rather you dated someone nearer your own age."

"Boys my age are yawns."

"Sorry, the answer is still no."

"Mom, it's a church event. There will be chaperones. It's not like it's a wild party or anything like that."

"Anna, I don't want you dating that boy. Period. End of subject. Got it?"

"You've never met him. How can you judge someone you don't even know?"

"I don't have to meet him. He's three years older ... in dog years, that's — really old."

"He's not a dog!"

"Subject closed. Do you have homework?"

Anna heaved a sigh. "You are so unfair."

Rose dismissed the criticism as Anna left the kitchen. Lately, more and more often their discussions ended in an argument with Anna walking away. Was this part of having a teenager, or was it part of an even deeper problem? Where was Joey when she needed him?

The pizza and Eric arrived simultaneously. Rose met the deliveryman at the door and paid him. Anna took the steaming cartons out of her hand, and Eric trailed his sister into the kitchen, lunging for a box. Before Rose could get ice in the glasses, the meal was in progress.

"What about prayer?"

"We said it to ourselves," Eric declared around a slice of hot pepperoni.

This is wrong. Life should be saner. Dinner is about sitting down together. Parents asking about their children's day. Prayer. Sharing. Like that would happen with Joey working late every night and the rest of us on such a hectic schedule.

"Next time, let's try saying it out loud."

"I thought God could hear prayer whether we say it out loud or in our heart." Eric gulped from his glass of Coke. "At least that's what you've always said."

She hated it when they quoted her words back to her. "So you were listening?"

"I listen." He reached for another slice of pizza. "Where are you going tonight?"

"Choir practice." He knew that, why would he ask?

His face was a blank mask. Anna pulled a string of cheese off her pizza and munched on it, avoiding Rose's eyes. What evil plot was she hatching?

"Are you going to make it to our school Christmas concert?" Her daughter's voice had a confrontational tone.

"Of course I'll be there. Why wouldn't I?"

Anna shrugged.

"Don't forget, Mr. Whitley is having parents' day for the science class," Eric reminded her. "Dad has to work so I know he won't be there, and I don't want to ride with Ben and his parents."

"I'll be there. Wouldn't miss it." She'd have to look at her calendar and see what she could juggle around. The offhand way Eric mentioned parents' day told her better than words that she'd better make it or have a good reason why not.

She'd make a point of being there.

Fifteen minutes later the kids dashed out the front door, late for their church Christmas program practice. The church bus was running and they'd voted to ride it instead of going with her.

Sighing, Rose dropped into a kitchen chair and put her hands on her throbbing forehead. Joey. She needed to talk to him about Anna and Nick Chalmers. She knew the subject would come up again, repeatedly. Anna had a way of manipulating her father's opinion, but not this time. Anna was not dating Nick Chalmers. The hall clock chimed, and she glanced at her watch. Fifteen minutes to get to choir practice.

Rose's cell phone rang as she was dabbing on lipstick. She checked the caller ID and decided to let it go to voice mail. Sue Barton, a member of their Sunday school family, was a dear, but a hopeless hypochondriac who liked to endlessly drone about her latest anticipated illness. No doubt she wanted to discuss Jean and Ken. Rose hesitated. She should answer. No. Focus, Rose. The choir director hated it when members were late. She'd have to call Sue back when she found a spare moment. She sprinted out the door, searching for her car keys in her purse.

Jean was at choir practice, head high and twin red spots burning her cheeks. Rose made a point of sitting beside her. "I've been meaning to call you."

Her friend glanced over and offered a wan smile. "I've been in and out. Did you need something?"

"No." Of course she didn't need anything. She would have called out of concern, but then time slipped away. "How's Ken?"

Jean's features softened. "You know men; they take these things better than we do."

Rose nodded. Joey was the Rock of Gibraltar in a crisis. If anything serious ever happened to him ... She dismissed the awful thought. Joey's heart was strong as a lion. She relished the twinge of relief, and then felt guilty that her life was great compared to Jean's. She'd make time to call and check on her more often. She *would*.

The choir members filed into their seats, and Linda Stoner distributed new music. As she stepped into the choir loft, Clay Lewis's walker tipped over. Linda stumbled, dropping her armload of music. The loose-leaf pages swirled up and around like a miniature snowstorm.

Clay was an irascible monkey, eighty-six and getting crabbier every day. He remained in the choir only because of the director's mercy. "Oops." He chuckled.

Linda ignored the teasing note, but Rose noticed the deep teeth indentations on her bottom lip.

The elderly man riffled through the sheet music. "What's wrong with the old songs? Can't abide this new caterwauling. Sounds like a pack of hens crowing."

"Hens don't crow." Linda handed him another sheet.

"And these new songs aren't music either."

Ah, Christmas—the spirit of joy, warm hearts, laughing faces. Rose leaned back in her chair, blocked out the noisy room, and thought about the nice hot bubble bath she was going to take when she got home.

After practice, Jade came up to her as she was getting ready to leave. "Rose, may I talk to you for a moment?"

"Sure, Jade. What's up?" *More buttonless donations? I'll scream! Shame on you, Rose. You're just tired.*

"Well, I gave a bag of clothing to the thrift shop. I was in a hurry, so I left the items by the front door."

"Ah. Was that you?" *Surely she didn't want the things back?*

Jade hesitated. "I don't know how to say this, it's so embarrassing."

"Is there anything I can do to help?" Rose asked her. She had a million things needing her attention at home, not to mention Joey.

Jade sighed. "I don't suppose a lot of people know this, but I'm taking care of my mother. She has Alzheimer's.

Eventually I'll have to put her in a home, but I'm trying to keep her as long as I can."

"I didn't know, Jade. I'm so sorry." Rose cringed. Did she walk around in a blind stupor? This was news to her.

"Yes, well, Mom found the clothes, and I didn't know until today that she had cut off all the buttons. I found them in a plastic bag in her nightstand."

Rose swallowed. *When will you learn, Rose? Never judge, not until you've walked a mile in another's shoes.*

"I wondered if I could give you the buttons, or maybe I could just take the clothes back and sew them on myself."

"Oh no, I can do it," Rose assured her. "Do you have the buttons with you?"

"Right here." Jade fished a plastic bag out of her purse. "I appreciate this so much, Rose. She can be a handful, but she's worth the trouble."

"I understand, really I do." They said good-night, and Rose watched as Jade made her way out of the church. Everyone had a story, a secret hurt. If she just wasn't so quick to think the worst ... Or fail to notice. Joey's earlier accusation rang in her ear, and she wondered if he was correct.

Later, while sugar cookies baked in the oven, Rose checked her email. She was on so many prayer and chat loops, it sometimes took hours to wade through them. Joey was sprawled in the recliner, comatose. She didn't want to disturb him. They needed to talk about Anna and this Chalmers kid, but it could wait. It would have to wait. Her husband was so exhausted, he wouldn't be coherent this time of night.

Rose sighed. How long had it been since she and Joey had spent time just talking? When they were first married, they could talk for hours about anything and everything. Then his business grew, they had kids, and suddenly there wasn't time anymore. She took a sheet of cookies out of the oven and transferred them to a cooling rack. A nagging thought felt like a pebble in her shoe, annoying, persistent. She'd had more time for family, for Joey, before she got so involved with volunteer work.

Lord, am I wrong? There was so much need in the world, surely God wanted her to do her share to help anywhere she could. And it sure seemed there was no end to the needs.

What do you want me to do?

She waited for a heavenly answer.

When she fell into bed three hours later, exhausted, she was still waiting.

advent

The Advent wreath is a popular symbol of the beginning of the church year. It is a circular evergreen wreath (real or artificial) with five candles, four around the wreath and one in the center. The colors of the candles vary with different traditions, but there are usually three purple or blue candles and one pink or rose candle.

"Girls' night out already?" Joey tried to pilfer a canapé off the tray Rose was finishing. She batted his fingers aside. "Hands off! You'll have to take the kids out for burgers tonight."

"Not again. Rose, I'm bushed. Isn't there a can of something in the house?"

Rose opened a cabinet and looked. "There's some Bac-Os and a can of hominy." She caught the hint of irritation in his groan and decided to ignore it. There really was no way she could miss this meeting. Linda would track her down and make her go. Women's night out made the week. Besides, they'd exchange gifts tonight, and she couldn't leave her person empty-handed.

She encased the tray of canapés in plastic wrap and stored it in the refrigerator while her husband stepped to the sink and picked around in the pieces of discarded cucumber shavings. "I was hoping for a roast chicken tonight."

She slammed the refrigerator door. "I'm sorry—I'm only one person! Can't you take the kids to McDonald's?" She aimed a kiss at his cheek on her way out. "By the time I shopped for the vegetables, crackers, pâté, and cheese, and put it all together, there wasn't time to start anything for dinner. I'll try to be home early, and don't let the kids touch the tray. It's for the deacon's meeting tomorrow night. Oh, and can you stop by the store on the way home and get milk?"

"I thought you were just at the store."

"I was, but I forgot milk. Better pick up a box of cereal too." She left before the conversation got more heated. She shoved Eric's bicycle out of the drive before she could back out.

Sliding the transmission into reverse, Rose cringed when she caught a brief glimpse of her husband standing at the kitchen window, eating a discarded cucumber slice.

Rose, you're neglecting your family.

Agreed, but it was Christmas, and Christmas came only once a year. After Christmas, she'd be a better wife. After the holiday, things would settle down, and she'd fix a roast with mashed potatoes, gravy, and sugar snap peas.

Seconds later she gunned the car, noting the dash clock. She was going to be *so* late.

Rose went straight home from the dinner and gift exchange to find Joey and the kids gone. He must have taken them someplace to eat after all. Now would be a good time to decorate the tree, to get that chore out of the way. *A chore?* She used to enjoy putting up the tree and hanging the sentimental ornaments. Now it was just one more thing on her to-do list.

She was hanging the last silver bow on the tree when she heard the garage door open. *Joey.* Simply saying his name felt good, reassuring. She tossed the last of the tinsel in the box and went to meet her family, greeting them with energetic hugs.

"What's all this?" Joey asked, trying to get in the doorway.

"I'm glad you're home." She leaned up and kissed him, then took the bag containing milk and cereal out of his hand. "I missed you."

"We went shopping." He drew her back for a more thorough greeting. When they were first married, they kissed like this every night. These days, a peck and a grunt were the norm. Taking his coat, she hung it in the closet. The kids trudged upstairs to call friends.

"How was the old hen's meeting?"

"Fun. We had a gift exchange. I got another candle."

He groaned. "The garage shelf won't hold another candle—it's about to fall now. Why don't you get rid of those things? You don't even like candles."

She grinned. "Convince my friends of that. We'll be the best equipped house on the block during a power outage."

He wandered into the living room where a fire blazed in the hearth. The tree, always a splendid sight, twinkled brightly in the front window. Rose mentally sighed, so grateful that for now, this moment, all was right in the world.

Joey reached for the paper and sat down in his recliner. She glanced at her watch, remembering the box of fresh holly sitting in the garage. She still had time to decorate the foyer before she would collapse into bed. She glanced at Joey, then back to the foyer. He seemed perfectly content—shoes kicked off, immersed in the stock report. Still, she tested the domestic waters.

"Honey? Do you care if I hang the holly in the foyer?" If he forbid her to do another thing tonight, she would respect his wishes.

"Umm?"

He didn't care. Rose exhaled and went to the garage with her newest addition to the candle collection. She paused on the bottom step, trying to shake the niggling thought that with all she did, she was as ineffective as a screen door on a submarine.

She sank to the step, letting the darkness swallow her. Scents of motor oil and dried grass mingled with the fresh holly. She could hear the ten o'clock news and the kids upstairs banging around when they should be getting ready for bed. The Bergmen household was a far cry from the Cleaver household. How did Ward and June do it? Keep a sane, orderly life, yet be strong, productive-minded community leaders? For a second, Rose thought about joining Joey. She'd remove his paper and glasses, sit on his lap, and just talk. They hadn't done that in a long time — just talk.

Dear God, why do I feel so worn, so empty, so tired? I spend every waking moment doing what I can, but my efforts amount to sifted chaff, they're meaningless. I try to keep people well fed, but it's their soul that's hungry. How do I nourish a soul with casseroles and cookies?

Wearily she got up and turned on the garage over-head light. She still had to take a casserole to Lois Monday night. Dragging a ladder to the candle shelf, she made the newest deposit. The white dove looked content perched with its peers.

On her way back into the house, she balanced the box of holly on her knee and tried to turn out the light. A sudden crash shattered the stillness.

Wincing, she called out, "Honey? The candle shelf just collapsed."

The first lighted Advent candle is traditionally the candle of Expectation or Hope (or in some traditions, Prophecy). This draws attention to the anticipation of the coming of a Messiah that weaves its way like a golden thread through Old Testament history. As God's people were abused by power-hungry kings, led astray by self-centered prophets, and lulled into apathy by halfhearted religious leaders, there arose a longing among some for God to raise up a new king who would show them how to be God's people. They yearned for a return of God's dynamic presence in their midst.

advent

Eric was quiet and withdrawn at breakfast late in the following week. Rose noticed Joey shooting him curious looks.

"You okay, buddy?"

"Yeah. I guess so."

"You sure?"

"He's upset because neither of you made it to the science class parents' day," Anna volunteered.

Rose paused with her forkful of scrambled eggs halfway to her mouth. She had completely forgotten.

Eric's eyes burned hot with anger. "You *promised*. I had to ride with Ben's parents."

"Oh my gosh! I had to take a dish by Lois's and I decided to do some last minute shopping ... Oh, Eric, I'm *so* sorry."

"Yeah. I'll bet you didn't forget any of your meetings." He shoved his chair back and bolted from the room.

Joey glanced up. "What science class parents' day? Why didn't you tell me about it?"

"I guess I didn't *mention* it because I knew you would be at work." Rose tried to defend herself, knowing full well she was in the wrong on this one. When did she become so defensive ... so edgy?

Anna sidled from the room.

Joey shook his head. "I would have gone if I'd known. The event was important to Eric." Silence encompassed the room as both Joey and Rose looked at one another. Joey continued, "So have you called Jean about Ken recently?"

"No ... not yet, but I will."

"You've been saying that for days. You'll feel better if you do it, Rose."

Rose flushed. She felt bad enough without him laying a guilt trip on her. "I'll call, okay?"

Joey dropped his napkin on the table and stood up. "Did you ever think you might need to ease up on some of these outside activities?"

She would have come up with a dandy retort, but he had already left the room.

Pushing back from the table, she grabbed up the breakfast dishes. Why was *she* the villain? How come the kids didn't blame their father for missed events?

Sinking back into the chair, she ran her fingers through her short cropped hair.

Rose couldn't shake her melancholy mood. Something was missing in her life, and she knew it as she later drove to the Christian Restoration Center. The volunteer work at the center was important to her. Someone had said that when a parent goes to prison, the whole family goes there too. This particular ministry worked with those behind bars, the at-risk families of those who were imprisoned, and ex-offenders once they were released. For the past three years, the church had helped with their Christmas program, wrapping gifts for the children of incarcerated parents.

Right now, Rose's heart felt heavy when she picked up four women at the church parking lot.

"Have you heard about Sue Barton?" Sharon rummaged in her purse and took out a stick of gum.

"She phoned the other night, but I was on my way out to choir practice. I haven't gotten back to her yet." Rose sat back to navigate the heavy morning traffic.

"She found a lump in her left breast."

Deafening silence filled the car. Not a woman spoke, but Rose's heart sank. Sue had found a *lump* in her breast? Was that why she had called? Her throat closed as she listened to the quiet speculations now floating around the interior of the car.

"Probably nothing—they say that 80 percent of all lumps are benign," one of the ladies commented hopefully.

Eighty percent of other women's lumps were benign, and that was a blessing. But what about the other 20 percent? Rose switched lanes, her ears tuned to the conversation.

"My sister found a lump last year. They did a biopsy and everything turned out fine."

"Sue's such a worrier," someone commented. "She stresses over everything."

A lump definitely qualified as "stress" in Rose's estimation. She would call Sue the moment she got home. Her headache that had been only an annoyance now began to expand and intensify. She hadn't made that luncheon date with Jean yet. She wondered how the family was doing. Had they heard anything from Ken's tests, or were they still in a perpetual frozen state waiting for the phone to ring?

And Blyth—she needed to pray for Blyth, but her mind was going in fifty different directions. Drawing a deep breath, Rose reminded herself of first things first. Wrap the presents for the inmates' children, and then worry about phone calls.

It was nearing three o'clock when she left the prison fellowship building. Her head felt like someone had ripped it off her shoulders and given it a couple of hard stomps. She dropped the other women off at their cars and headed home, wondering what to do about dinner. She couldn't send Joey and the kids out again. She still had a sea of pending tasks ahead of her and not a leftover in the refrigerator.

As she drove along the highway, the exit to Dr. Reel's office came in sight. Before she realized it, she threw on the blinker. Five minutes later, she walked into the clinic, unannounced and with no appointment.

The receptionist glanced up, smiling. "Rose?" Her gaze dropped to the appointment sheet. "I don't have you scheduled."

"I don't have an appointment." Rose sagged against the small reception window, aware that she probably looked as wiped out as she felt. "Is it possible to see the doctor? My head feels like it's about to explode, and I've already used my Maxalt for the month." She thought of the empty blister packs in the bathroom cabinet and wanted to weep. Insurance paid for only so many a month, and she had a lot of month left.

"Rose?" Dr. Reel's nurse, Lana, spotted her and stepped to the window. "What's going on?"

"I'm out of Maxalt and on impulse I stopped, hoping the doctor can work me in."

Lana winked. "I think it's possible."

Ten minutes later Rose climbed onto the obligatory scale. "I have to weigh for Maxalt?"

Chuckling, Lana jotted Rose's current weight on the chart. "Are you dieting?"

"Me?" She laughed. She could eat anything that didn't eat her first and never gain a pound. "I forget to eat most days."

Lana sobered. "I know we're all under a lot of stress this time of year. You need to get plenty of rest and eat healthy. It's important to take care of ourselves. Makes those trips to the doctor further apart and your Maxalt last longer."

Dr. Reel breezed in, greeting Rose warmly. She had been his patient since she was much younger, and he knew the origin of every nick and abrasion on her. "Rose, Rose, hair of blonde," he teased as his eyes scanned her chart. "You've lost five pounds since your last visit. Why is that?"

She smiled and shrugged, bracing for the lecture. "I'm too busy to eat."

"Still doing all that volunteer work?"

"Some of it, yes." What was this? Had Joey called him? No. He wouldn't have a way of knowing she would stop by today. It had been purely a reflexive inquiry.

Dr. Reel shook his head. "There's only so much one person can do. Set your limits and stick with them. Slow down, write yourself notes about eating, and hang them around your neck." He winked. "You're ten pounds below the norm—don't lose anymore. Now, Lana tells me you've used all of your Maxalt—when was your last refill?"

"Two weeks ago."

He shook his head, doing a basic examination of the type doctors are required to do.

"Migraines getting worse?"

"Not worse, but more frequent." Lately it seemed she was threatened with one every day.

"Got to slow down, young lady." He patted her knee and sat down on a rolling stool.

By the time she left, Rose had something to get her through the headaches until she could refill her present prescription.

"These pills are no substitute for rest and setting a slower pace," Dr. Reel told her. "I'm suggesting relaxation exercises and a multivitamin to nudge your appetite."

On the way out, Rose stopped Lana and thanked her for getting her in so quickly.

Humming "God Rest Ye Merry Gentlemen," Rose tooled home down the freeway that was heavily congested with rush-hour traffic. *Call Sue!* Her mind instructed her. She could multitask, and if she called now, she wouldn't forget it. She fumbled in her purse for her cell phone. Her groping fingers found her wallet, notepad, pen, flashlight—a flashlight? Why would she have a flashlight in her purse? Frustrated, she upended the purse, dumping the contents onto the seat. A quick glance at the mess—and that's what it was—revealed the phone, and she snatched it up, then swerved back into her own lane. Traffic was moving fast and she had to keep up with it. It was dangerous to take her eyes off the road.

What was Sue's number? Four, seven, six, no that wasn't right. The car in front of her braked for a turn. Rose slammed on the brakes, dropping the phone. She leaned over, stretching for it, her fingers barely brushing the smooth metal. Just a tiny bit further. Her head dipped below the dash for a second and her hand closed around the phone, just as squealing tires and blaring horns jerked her erect.

She whipped the wheel sharply to the right, narrowly avoiding sideswiping an oncoming car. A cacophony of bleating horns and rude gestures confronted her. She quickly hit the blinker and eased to the shoulder.

Shaken, she rested her hand on her hammering chest, appalled at the highway disaster she'd nearly created. The pain in her head kept sync with her pounding heart.

Braking in the garage fifteen minutes later, she bowed her head. *Thank you, God, for watching over me.* Motorists were nuts! What was it about the holidays that brought out the crazies? Present company excepted, of course.

advent

FRANCE
Joyeux Noël

The crèche (manger scene) occupies a place of prominence in the French home. The bûche de Noël, a log-shaped cake, has become a favorite Christmas delicacy. Children leave their shoes by the fireside on Christmas Eve, hoping Père Noël (Father Christmas) will fill them with gifts before morning. Their parents attend Christmas masses at midnight and return to a late supper known as Réveillon. On Epiphany Eve, three figures are added to the crèche in celebration of the visit of the magi.

The minute she entered the house and saw the smirk on her fifteen-year-old daughter's face, she knew something was wrong. Eric slumped on the living room sofa, while his father stood above him, glowering.

"What's up?"

"Tell your mother what's up, Eric."

Eric's flushed features turned even more sullen. He shifted, refusing to meet Rose's questioning eyes.

She laid her purse on the hall table. "What?" It couldn't be too bad. Eric was here, looking perfectly normal. No broken bones or telltale gashes. Anna appeared to be in an excellent mood ... Uh-oh. Trouble.

"Eric," Joey prompted.

Eric spat out the confession. "I was smoking in the school bathroom."

Rose wasn't certain she'd heard correctly. "What?"

"He was caught *smoking* in the school bathroom," Joey repeated. "Our son. Our *son*. Caught smoking in the bathroom."

Rose sank into a chair, her head reeling. "Smoking?"

"In the bathroom."

Their son firmed his lips, but his sullen appearance didn't change.

"Look at me, Eric," Rose implored. "What were you thinking? You never behave like this."

Eric flared. "I might as well! No one cares what I do, anyway."

"That's not true, Eric—of course we care." He couldn't really feel like that. He couldn't. She reeled from the suppressed anger in his expression.

"You *promised* to come to parents' day, and I tried to remind you, but you were too busy to listen."

When had he tried to remind her? She couldn't remember. Had she actually ignored him in her quest to get the casserole delivered to Lois while it was still hot? Whether she had or not, Eric felt like she had, and that was what mattered.

She closed her eyes and then opened them to find Joey staring at her, his face flushed. "I've been trying to tell you that you're doing too much. You're not even home long enough to know what your children are doing."

"You're blaming *me*?" Where was he coming from, this man who worked late every night and left the children's whereabouts up to her?

"That's right. The kids need you."

"And what about you?" She lobbed the accusation right back at him. Two could play the blame game. "You spend every waking moment at work. Let me remind you that you're the head of this house. Your children need you too."

Joey straightened, hands braced on his hips. "Don't try to make me feel guilty about working. I have to, if the bills are to be paid."

Rose stared at him, her mouth working like a beached fish.

"Stop arguing! You guys used to *never* argue!" Eric shouted.

"Go to your room, Eric. Your mother and I will be up shortly to talk to you." Eric shoved the chair aside and left the room.

"Joey, you shouldn't speak to Eric in that tone." It was bad enough that he snarled at her, but to talk like that to his son, and in front of Anna ...

"Rose, wake up! Our son was caught smoking in the bathroom. This is only the start. Unless we get a firm grip on this, we can expect more incidents. This one might be insignificant, but the next time it could be drugs."

Drugs. Blyth flashed through her mind, and for a second, she understood the near panic Blyth was feeling.

Joey stormed out of the room, leaving Rose with a biting headache and guilt the size of Mount Everest on her shoulders.

She leaned back in the chair, speechless. The cheerily twinkling Christmas tree and freshly hung holly suddenly looked mockingly pathetic. *Dear Lord...* She couldn't finish the prayer. Her ideal family was rapidly going down the drain.

Rose sat two sheep on the shelf calendar along with the date, December 15. Ten days until Christmas, and no one had offered to have the yearly Christmas Eve dinner. She suspected that her sister and two sisters-in-law expected her to host again; she had for the past four years. Not that she minded, but maybe this year they'd take the stress off her.

She sank onto a kitchen stool and pulled the book holding her call-often numbers toward her. Family, friends, and business numbers all here at her fingertips. Organization was her middle name. This year she would politely but firmly insist that her sister or sisters-in-law take over. Her moving finger stopped at Jo, her sister-in-law who was always saying they were going to get a larger house but never did. Rose punched in the number and started counting rings. At six she was ready to hang up, when Jo came on the line, voice harried.

"Jo? Hi! It's Rose."

"Rose! I was just thinking about you." Her sister-in-law had that warm tone—the one in which she was about to excuse herself. "Hold on a sec. I just walked in the door." The line went silent, then Jo returned. "Tell me why every year I wait until the last minute to do my Christmas shopping. The checkout lines are murder! I was stepped on twice and my feet are killing me. It's a madhouse out there!"

Drawing a deep breath, Rose took the plunge. "Remember when we all agreed that Mom and Dad are getting too old to host a gathering of what—nineteen or twenty of us, and I agreed to have the dinner at my house that year?"

"More like twenty-four of us. I'm pretty sure we'll have an assortment of girlfriends and boyfriends there this year."

Rose smiled, then sobered. Boyfriends? Would Anna want to invite Nick Chalmers? She was still obsessing over his New Year's Eve invitation.

"Jo, four years ago, we decided to split the hostess duties, and I was wondering if you'd take this year." There. That was in-your-face, but she wasn't feeling particularly discreet. Just dragged through a wringer.

"Oh. I know we did, and I was hoping that we'd have a bigger house by now, or that we'd at least built on, but they're cutting back at the plant and Stan's been leery to do anything."

Rose's brother was a worrywart. He had been living with the fear of plant cutbacks for the last fifteen years.

"We'd be all over each other here," Jo reminded.

Rose cleared her throat. Jo's house was smaller than hers, but adequate. So they'd be crowded. Not many households could seat twenty-four comfortably.

A huge sigh from Jo warned what was coming. "Would you care to have it again this year? I really don't think I'm able to cook for that many people, and I know I couldn't possibly fix the *lutefisk*."

"I'll bring the lutefisk and the lefse." The traditional dishes were Grandpa and Grandma's favorites at holiday gatherings. It wouldn't be Christmas without some of the old customs. Rose sweetened the offer. "I'll even bake *sirupsnipper*—dozens, if you'll have the dinner."

"Oh, you *know* how much I love that cookie, but I'm having my family on Christmas Day," Jo argued. "We're a smaller group, and two huge meals back to back would be more than I can handle. Can you have it? Do you mind?"

Rose's defenses began to crumble. Her usual mantra, *I guess I could* rose to her lips, and she bit back the words. Not this time. "Yes, I do mind. I'm buried right now. I'll help cook, but I've had the dinner the past four years. It really is someone else's turn."

"What about Jamie? I'm sure she'll be glad to do it."

And pigs could line dance. Her sister would find every excuse on record to avoid having the dinner without outright telling everyone to stay home. Rose made some sort of comment about checking with Jamie—and hung up. She reviewed the list of telephone numbers, considering and rejecting names until there wasn't anyone left but Jamie.

She chewed the end of her pen. She'd force Jamie to have it. She wouldn't let up until she agreed. After all, Jamie was family and should take her turn. True, Rose had protected, advised, spoiled, and covered for her adorable baby sister until it had become a habit. But Jamie was grown now with a family of her own, and it was past time she stepped up to the plate. The Christmas dinner plate.

She dialed the number and Jamie picked up promptly. "Hello."

"Hi, Jamie."

"Oh, Rose. I bought your present today. Have you bought mine?" she teased.

"Bought, wrapped, and hid in a hole in the backyard." Jamie could ferret out the most well kept secret, especially if it concerned her.

"If I guess what it is, will you tell me?"

"No. Don't even try."

"Oh, come on. You didn't used to be so mean."

She was about to get as mean as it got. "Hey kiddo, I'm calling about Christmas Eve dinner."

"Sure thing. What do you want me to bring?"

Your house. "I was hoping you'd host it this year. Mom and Dad aren't able to, and Jo's house is too small."

"It's bigger than mine!"

"I know—convince Jo. So, how about it? Can we come to your house this year?"

Please, please, please. One year—one magnificent year where I bring a veggie tray and enjoy the holiday.

"Oh, I would, but I get so ding-dong nervous with all those people milling around. I couldn't possibly contend with twenty people."

"Twenty-four. Jo reminded me there'll be girlfriends and boyfriends this year. Our children are growing up."

"Is Anna bringing that cute guy she wants to date?"

"No. Nick Chalmers is too old for her." And just how did her sister know about Nick Chalmers? Had Anna been calling her? Confiding in her?

"How many did you say?" Jamie asked. "What's the full count?"

"Twenty-four—maybe more."

"Well, there you are." Jamie's tone sounded so convincing, even Rose could see the wisdom. "My nerves would be shot. Have you asked Jo?"

"She's having her family Christmas Day. Thinks it would be too much to have two big back-to-back meals."

"Oh yes—it would be hard. Look, I'm really sorry. You know I'd do it if I could. How about I bring two dishes? Would that help?"

Yeah. And bring a vacuum, eight hours of prep work, another couple of hours to wash the Christmas china and polish silverware, a thirty-pound turkey, and ... Valium. That should cover it.

She sighed. *Rose, Rose. Your Christmas spirit is slipping. Plummeting, Lord. Plunging. I love my family. Christmas is special, but I've come to dread the extra work.* The realization was like ice water dashed in her face.

Rose remembered the Christmas Eve Jamie had shown up empty-handed, and when asked what she'd brought, she said a big appetite.

"What about Charlene?" Rose threw out the suggestion.

Jamie hooted. "You can't be serious. Charlene cook Christmas dinner for twenty-four people and get it on the table before New Year's?"

"No, probably not." Rose adored her younger brother, Eddy, and his bride of one year was a charming girl, but she had yet to boil a wiener without bloating it. She recalled the time she had offered to share recipes with Charlene. The girl had batted her big brown eyes and looked rather vacant.

"What's stuffing?"

Good thing for Eddy, the bloom was still on the rose and food was not an issue with the man. He thought anything Charlene said or did was incredibly brilliant, puffy hot dogs included.

"Look, Rose." Jamie interrupted her thoughts. "I'm sorry, but someone is at the door. I'll have to call you back."

A click and Rose was alone, holding the receiver. She sighed. Face it, Rose. You're going to host Christmas Eve again this year. Her mind skipped to the anticipated evening, the most sacred of the year.

The family would arrive early. Once everyone was assembled, they would eat the traditional turkey and gravy, and then they would troop off to the early Christmas candlelight service.

Afterwards, the rush home, and then all would move to the living room for Scandinavian traditions — cookies and coffee and then the gift exchange.

Around ten or eleven, the family would track through mounds of discarded wrapping paper and begin filtering out, carrying armloads of gifts and empty casserole dishes. There would be a flurry of Christmas wishes, warm hugs, and gratitude for another successful family get-together.

When the door closed, Rose would set to work in the kitchen restoring order, washing and putting away dishes.

The kids would dispose of the mounds of used wrapping paper, and Joey would man the vacuum, a large can of RugDoctor, Windex, and a roll of paper towels. Every year, someone inevitably spilled food on the carpet, usually something ugly and tomato-based and nearly impossible to get out.

Then Eric and Anna would wander off to their rooms, and the televised Christmas mass would be over by the time she and Joey wearily climbed the stairs for bed. Wishing each a merry Christmas, they would drop an exhausted, misplaced kiss on the opposite pillow, and pass out.

Rose couldn't think of a single thing she wanted this Christmas other than a week of sheer nothing. Stay home, enjoy her family. Be lazy. Maybe not even change out of her bathrobe and fuzzy house slippers.

The phone rang and Rose reached for it, squelching a faint hope that Jamie or Jo had second thoughts. Joey's voice greeted her. "Hi, what's going on?"

"Not much, why?" She'd wait until evening to break the news that they were having Christmas dinner again. Not that he cared. He had plenty of Christmas spirit even if Rose's was drained.

"Wanted to warn you not to wait dinner for me tonight. I've got a late shipment going out and I'm stuck here."

She felt emptiness well up inside, a lonely void. He worked so hard; he should be home, by the fire with her . . .

only she wouldn't be here either. Tonight she had to attend the Sunday school Christmas party.

"Rose, you there?"

"I'm here. That's okay. I'll leave something for you to eat."

"Don't bother. I'll get a sandwich later."

"Okay, if that works." Maybe tomorrow she could fix that roast. With her luck, no one would be home to eat it.

"You sound sort of down, hon." Joey said. "I'm sorry we've been short with each other. Forgive me?"

"Sure. I talked to Jo and Jamie today."

"Oh yeah? What about? Christmas dinner?"

She could tell from his voice that somehow her tone had given her away. "We're hosting again."

"Couldn't talk Jamie or Jo into taking it, huh?

How well he knew her family. "They both had believable excuses."

"Don't worry about it. The two of us can handle the dinner. Christmas only comes once a year."

"Joey, tonight's the class party. Can't you get away a little early and stop by the Millers' house on your way home?"

"Christmas party? Oh hon, the party completely slipped my mind." She heard papers rattle. "I'll do what I can, Rose.

"It's Christmas, Joey." But she knew work didn't stop for the holidays.

"Hon, I would if I could, but business has picked up, which is good, but it means more work for me, and right now I'm swamped. You go and have fun. I'll try to wrap it up early, but I can't promise."

"I'd have more fun if you were there." Everything was more fun with Joey by her side. Besides, being half a couple wasn't any fun.

"I'm sorry, Rose. I'd be there if I could, but when you run your own business, it's not always easy to walk away."

Guilt. Joey worked so hard to provide for them. How could she make it harder for him all because of a Christmas party? *Where are your priorities, Rose?*

Tears welled in her eyes. He was a good man. And reportedly, good men were hard to find. She had to take better care of him. If he couldn't make the party, she wouldn't say a word.

Magnanimous of you, Rosie.

Well, she was sorta in a magnanimous mood.

advent

The third candle, usually for the Third Sunday of Advent, is traditionally pink or rose, and symbolizes Joy at the coming Advent of the Christ. Sometimes the colors of the sanctuary and vestments are also changed to rose for this Sunday. However, increasingly in many churches, the pink Advent candle is used on the fourth Sunday to mark the joy at the impending Nativity of Jesus.

Judy Thomas phoned as Rose was leaving the house. "Just wanted to let you know that Sue's biopsy came back benign."

Rose closed her eyes with relief. "That's wonderful news."

"Isn't it? I can't think of a better Christmas present."

Neither could she. "Thanks for letting me know, Judy. I'll call Sue and tell her how relieved I am."

"There is much to be thankful for. Have a great day, Rose, and take care."

Rose hung up and immediately dialed Sue's number. "I just heard the good news. Judy called."

Sue's voice rang with relief. "I'm praising the Lord. I can't tell you the agony I went through. I thought of everything imaginable."

"It must have been a difficult few days."

She paused. Apologizing didn't get any easier, no matter how long you procrastinated.

"Sue, I've been intending to call and check on you, but somehow I never got around to it. I'm so sorry I wasn't there to help you through the awful time."

Silence followed, enough to let Rose know Sue had noticed her absence. "That's all right, Rose. I know how busy you are."

"I prayed for you." Rose offered a crumb, all she had.

"A lot of people prayed for me, and I appreciate every one. You know, I could actually feel those prayers enveloping me like a warm blanket, but I guess that sounds cheesy."

"No, it doesn't. We do feel the love and support of those who care about us, and I do care for you, Sue."

"I know that, Rose. I never doubted it."

Rose felt as if a load had been lifted from her shoulders. Sue always made the difficult easy. "Tell you what. Let's go to lunch sometime soon and celebrate."

"Why, I'd love that. Thank you, Rose, and thank you for calling."

She hung up, promising herself to keep the date, but admittedly it would have to be after the holidays.

Thankfully, Sue's crisis was over, which removed some of the urgency. A pity life was so hectic. She needed to call Jean. She'd kept up with Ken's reports through snatched conversations at church. The tests were still inconclusive, and Ken and Jean would spend this holiday worrying, waiting.

Hosting the annual family Christmas Eve dinner suddenly didn't seem so dreadful.

Class members Nina and Paul Miller's house pulsated with twinkling lights racing through every shrub and bare tree branch when Rose arrived for the party.

Mrs. Claus in person — Nina Miller in costume — opened the door. "Rose! Merry Christmas! Joey's not with you?"

"Merry Christmas. No, he had to work late."

She made a face. "That's too bad, we'll miss him. Give me your coat. The food's over there. Make yourself at home."

Nina turned to welcome new guests, and Rose stripped out of her coat. She headed straight for the dessert table to fill a plate before she began to mingle. She gazed from one delightful dessert to another, suddenly grateful for her ten-pound weight deficit. Everything looked and smelled delicious, and she wanted to try it all.

Lois Gleeson openly compared her scant plate with Rose's selection. "I'll be glad when I can eat like that again."

Rose eyed Lois's plate. "Looks like you're doing all right for someone who recently had her gall bladder removed."

Lois laughed. "I'll survive, but my appetite's slow to return."

"Other than being calorie deprived, how are you?"

"I'm doing okay. Thank you again for all the lovely food you brought. It was such a blessing. Christmas isn't an ideal time to have surgery."

Rose agreed. She didn't know what she would do if some emergency arose. So many people depended on her for holiday magic.

"Since I was forced to slow down, I've realized most of the things that I thought were important, aren't. From now on I'm going to live at a slower pace," Lois said.

"Take time to pick the daisies?" If only she'd heed the advice and stop running around like a chicken with its head cut off.

She cared with all her heart.

"You got it." Lois pointed her fork at Rose. "What about you? Are you feeling all right?

Rose lifted a brow. "I'm fine, why do you ask?"

"You look pale, and I don't remember those dark circles under your eyes being quite so prominent."

Rose stared at her, slightly offended.

Lois softened the observation. "I'm just asking because I'm concerned."

"That's nice of you, Lois, but I'm feeling just fine. As soon as Christmas is over, I'll slow down." At least that's what she kept telling herself.

"I'm not trying to pry," Lois said, bending closer. "But you just don't look well, and it worries me."

"I'm fine. Tired, rushed, ready for Christmas to be over, but fine."

Lois frowned. "Christmas is so special."

"Yes, I'm sorry. I guess I'm a little cranky tonight."

As soon as she could, Rose made her excuses and wandered away. Surely she didn't look that bad. She'd been congratulating herself on the weight loss, and Lois made her sound like she had one foot in the grave and the other on a grease spot.

Nina wandered by, obviously having overheard the exchange. "She doesn't mean to be rude."

"I know." Rose sat the plate aside, appetite vanished. She pushed back a strand of hair and winced when she caught a glimpse of her reflection in the festively decorated mirror hanging over the mantel. Maybe Lois wasn't that far off after all. She did look like a well-worn shoe.

"Have you seen Blyth?" Rose asked. Nina and Blyth were friends, not just the see-you-in-church kind of friends, but bosom buddies.

"She's not here. I suppose you know Frank is giving her a hard time right now."

"She mentioned something about it. I'm so sorry for her ... can I help? Does she need anything?"

Nina shook her head. "That boy was the cutest thing when he was little. I never thought he'd turn out like this ... driving Blyth nuts, doing drugs."

Rose didn't know what to say. She merely nodded.

"He lost his father, that was a blow, and then he started running around with the wrong crowd. One thing led to another."

Rose bit her lip, thinking of Eric. Would someone, someday, say something like this about her son? Not if she could help it. But then she supposed Blyth had thought the same thing once. There was no magic formula, no crystal ball when raising children. *Teach them the decrees and laws, and show them the way to live and the duties they are to perform.* Had Rose done that for her children, or had she been too busy?

advent

The center Advent candle is white and is called the Christ Candle. It is traditionally lighted on Christmas Eve or Day. Many churches light it on the Sunday preceding Christmas, with all five candles continuing to be lighted in services through Epiphany (January 6).

10

December twenty-fourth. Christmas Eve. Winter arrived in the Twin Cities. A thin sheen of ice coated branches and shrubs. Rose was standing at the stove when Joey entered the kitchen dressed for work. She sat a pitcher of orange juice on the table and glanced at him. "Where are you going?"

He had the grace to look guilty. "I've got a couple of hours' work to catch up on. Thought I'd go in early and get it out of the way."

"You *promised* to help me with dinner preparations."

"Hey, I will. Just give me time, and I'll be here," he snapped.

"I don't have time." Rose slapped a plate of bacon on the table. "I cannot believe this. Christmas Eve, and you have to work."

"I'm not running out on you, I'll be back in time to help."

"I'm holding you to the promise, Joey." She slammed a skillet on the burner and jacked up the flame.

Suddenly she whirled around, marched to the refrigerator, and jerked open the door. Her eyes scanned the shelf where she had stashed the groceries she'd bought for the family dinner. The tubs of dip and ingredients for appetizers were missing.

"I'm going to throttle someone."

"What?" Joey turned to look, wide-eyed.

"Someone's eaten the stuff I bought for the dinner tonight. Now, I have to go to the store!"

Joey swallowed the last of his coffee and made a break for the door. "Two hours. That's all, I promise." He sent a kiss in her direction. "Grouch."

Rose threw a dishcloth at him as he disappeared into the garage. The door closed and she turned off the burner, grabbed a notepad and pen, and sat down in the breakfast nook to start on a revised grocery list, ear tuned to a local disk jockey's weather report.

"Overnight freezing rain has left parking lots and sidewalks coated in ice, but the roads are clear. Don't worry, kids! It'll take more than a cold rain to scare Santa away from the Twin Cities!"

Downing the last of her coffee, Rose got up and began the day—her busiest of the year. The family was scheduled to arrive around five, and she didn't expect to take a deep breath until long after midnight.

She woke up Anna and Eric and gave them chores to do, confident they'd go back to sleep as soon as she left. Clutching her grocery list, the grouch headed out to the van.

"Cream cheese, oranges, cheese in a jar, celery." She repeated the glossary as she swung the car into the busy shopping complex. Eric and Anna were on vacation until the first of the year, so there wasn't any frantic rush to get them fed and off to school. Maybe they would be up and working when she got home. Then again, maybe not.

From the looks of the empty cart area, the store was a madhouse. Grabbing the first available basket, she wheeled toward the front door. The parking lot was an ice rink. She inched along, careful to watch where she stepped, trying to avoid getting run over by cars backing out of parking places. Suddenly her cart veered east and her body west.

In a hail of exploding stars, she sprawled on the icy lot, her head spinning. A man getting out of his vehicle slammed the car door and rushed to her aid.

"Lie still. I'm a doctor," he assured her.

Humiliated, she lay back while he respectfully probed for broken bones.

"How clumsy of me." Her head whirled. The fall had jarred every bone in her body. She cupped her right hand against her stomach and then wished she hadn't from the sudden stab of hot pain she felt in her wrist.

"I don't think anything's broken," he announced. "But you've taken a hard fall." He eased her to a sitting position.

By now others were staring as they grabbed carts and steered around her.

"Thank you, God," she murmured. A fall that hard could have caused considerable damage. She'd been lucky, but her right arm ached all the way to her shoulder.

"Do you want me to call someone or an ambulance? That was a nasty spill."

"I'm okay, really." If her spine was split down the middle, she couldn't afford a spare moment. She had a dinner to prepare. Thanking the good Samaritan for his doctoring skills, she held tightly to her cart, using it as a crutch, and entered the packed store. The shelves already looked as though they had been stripped by locusts. Shoppers and carts jammed the aisles. Frantic mothers with feisty toddlers tried to shop and pacify fretful babies at the same time.

Rose quickly located her items, but by the time she stood in the checkout lane, her right wrist hurt so badly that she was near tears. The cashier totaled the items and Rose wrote out the check left-handed. Her sacker wheeled the groceries out to the car and put them in the trunk. She eased in behind the wheel, bumping her wrist in the process. Pain, agonizing and razor sharp radiated through her, followed by a wave of nausea. For one horrible moment, she thought she would throw up. She couldn't drive home like this. What if she had an accident? Fumbling in her purse for her cell phone, she fought the urge to put her head on the steering wheel and bawl. Awkwardly using her left hand, she dialed Joey's phone. He answered on the first ring, and at the sound of his voice, she burst into tears.

"Rose?"

"Oh, Joey." She couldn't finish.

"Rose? Honey? Are you all right?" Alarm radiated through his tone.

"I fell in the grocery parking lot." She choked on a sob.

"You're hurt?"

"I think I broke my wrist. I can't drive."

"I'll be right there."

He hung up, and she breathed a prayer of relief. Joey was on his way. He'd take care of her. Minutes later he arrived, and their next-door neighbor, Mike O'Hara, pulled in behind him.

Joey opened the car door and helped her out, pulling her into a tight embrace. "It's okay, honey. Let's get you to a doctor."

Mike reached into the car and handed Rose her purse. "I'm taking your car home. I'll have my wife bring me back for my car."

"The trunk is full of groceries. Ninety-five dollars worth, too much to let ruin," Rose told him.

"The kids can take care of them." Joey held her arm, gently moving her to his car. Once he had her settled, he settled in on the driver's side and reached for his phone. Rose heard his half of the conversation.

"Your mother's been hurt. I'm taking her to the emergency room."

Pause.

"She's going to be okay, but Mike's bringing the car home. The trunk is full of groceries. You and Eric get them inside and put them away. I'll phone you from the emergency room."

Rose leaned her head back against the seat and closed her eyes. She could relax. Joey was in control.

Her mind shifted from reality to the absurd; it was Christmas Eve. She had a million and one things to do. She did not have time for a medical emergency. She hadn't put the turkey in the oven, a turkey that required at least seven hours to bake. The kids were home alone. Anna was old enough to take over, but would she? Rose realized she had never taken the time to impress upon Anna the importance of household responsibilities. Today was not the best time to start. It was Christmas Eve! She couldn't disappoint her family.

The emergency room was full. Evidently half the town had fallen on the ice. Something about a waiting room stymied her ability to converse. Maybe because there was such a lack of privacy. Her wrist hurt too much to hold a magazine, so she sat quietly, watching the minutes, precious minutes, tick by. So much to do. How would she get to it all?

Rose sighed. "Why today of all days? How am I going to get everything done before the family arrives?"

Joey patted her hand. "Don't worry. I'll take care of it."

She squinted at him. The man didn't have a clue what all was involved. He'd be as helpless in the kitchen as a monkey with a fat crayon.

He caught her expression.

"What?"

"You're going to fix the turkey and dressing?"

He grinned. "Sure. Why not?"

She raised her eyebrows. Why not? She snickered. At least the cookies were baked, cranberry salad ready, cornbread crumbled for the dressing. Check. Still, so much remained to be done.

"Dinner will be ruined. Anna can't cook anything but boxed macaroni and cheese—and maybe a brownie mix. I should have taken more time to teach her how to prepare a holiday meal."

"Rose?" The emergency room nurse peered around the door. "The doctor can take you now."

Joey helped Rose to her feet, and she headed for the doorway. When she turned to look at Joey, he was reaching for his cell phone. "I'm calling the kids. I'll be with you in a moment."

Two and a half hours later, he supported her weight and led her into their bedroom. "Easy, hon, easy." In seconds, she was tucked into bed, engulfed in a thickening fog.

"Are they sure my wrist isn't broken?"

"You heard the doctor. Severely sprained, but not broken. Ankle sprained ... a few bruises."

"Everything feels broken. I ache all over."

"You took a nasty fall, it's no wonder you're sore. Lie back and let the pain medication do its job."

She struggled to throw off the blanket and spread. "Have to get the turkey in the oven, peel potatoes, make stuffing."

Her husband gently pressed her back to the pillow. "You're not going anywhere right now."

"Joey!"

"Stay, Rose! The pain medication has knocked you for a loop. You're down for the count, girl. Now lie still and rest."

"But the turkey—"

"The turkey is in the oven." He readjusted the blanket, snapping it briskly into place.

"How'd it get there?" She realized how silly she sounded. Did she think it had flown into the oven? Anna had risen to the occasion. Bless her sweet heart.

"Anna's got it under control. She called Jamie for instructions."

Oh brother. "Jamie? *She* knows how to cook a turkey?" She'd never shown any inclination to cook one before.

Christmas was ruined. Without her, the family was help-less. *I'm so sorry I was so clumsy, Lord.*

"Anna can cook if she wants to. Give her a chance to show you what she can do. She might surprise you."

Maybe, but she practically had to beg her daughter to feed the cat.

Rose sensed her husband's frustration. "Are you angry at me?" she asked him.

"Not angry, Rose. Frustrated." Sighing, he sat down on the edge of the bed and ran a hand through his hair. He looked tired, so very tired. Why hadn't she noticed the worry lines around his eyes earlier?

"With me? I slipped on the ice, Joey. I know I should have put the turkey in the oven before I left, but I wasn't going to be gone more than half an hour."

"You're lucky you haven't hit the wall sooner." He rose from the bed and started to pace the carpet. "Good grief, haven't you noticed? This house has turned into a three-ring circus. We never sit down for a meal together—our basic vocabulary to the kids is, 'Hurry. Get in the car. We're going to be late.' We race around like fools, doing for everyone but ourselves."

"Anyone can slip and fall," she said.

"You do too much, Rose. Your lifestyle is an accident looking for a place to happen. Let someone else experience the blessing of helping out. You're hogging it all."

Hogging? She blunted his criticism by jerking the blanket over her head with her left hand. How dare he condemn her for wanting to make the holiday season perfect, for wanting to serve God and others throughout the year? Yes, she was busy, too busy. But what woman today with a family and social and church activities wasn't busy? Was he equating her fall as punishment for family neglect? She was grocery shopping when the accident happened, not idly sitting in a teahouse nibbling on crumpets with her friends!

He yanked the blanket off her head. "Rose, this has got to stop. Does the president have to declare National Eat-a-Meal-Together Day before this family slows down enough to examine our priorities?"

He had never spoken to her in this tone, not ever. The holiday madness was getting to him.

"Life will slow down, eventually. Christmas is here and I've finished the shopping, the wrapping. Almost everything is done."

He paused, turning to face her. "Rose, Jesus preached a simple 'religion.' Forgiveness, loving one's enemy, service from the heart, not done out of guilt or obligation. Man has chosen to put his own spin on the matter." His features softened. "We need to get back to the basics, hon. Home. Family. Time spent together building souls that will last for eternity, not for another meeting. I'm lonely. I *miss* you. Come home to me, Rose."

He missed her? She'd neglected him that badly? Tears swelled to her eyes. "You could have told me that you resent the time I spend on volunteer activities."

Was the lack of communication between them a symptom or a cause of a harried life?

"I did tell you, you just didn't listen. But it isn't just church activities, it's everything. Our son was caught smoking in the school bathroom. Our son, Rose. We stood in front of God and promised to rear him to the best of our abilities. Maybe if we weren't both gone all the time, Eric would have made a better choice."

"He knows better than to smoke."

"He knows his parents are so preoccupied trying to do good that they're never around when he needs them. Maybe he would discuss his problems with us if we were available, but we're always due at some meeting or function to serve others. Well what's wrong with serving our own, Rose? What's so wrong with nurturing, devoting every single day, not just a skimpy portion of it, to the very souls we brought into this world?"

Hot tears coursed down her cheeks. Everything he said was true, but wasn't he accusing her unfairly? She had lived on the fast track so long, she didn't know if she had jumped rail. God had blessed them so abundantly— surely she was obligated to give back? How did she get off the gerbil wheel? Surely this busyness wasn't his plan, but how else did she make her life count?

Sighing, Joey eased back down on the bed. She groaned with sweet relief when he began to gently massage her back, carefully kneading the bruised tissue. "I'm not blaming you; we're both at fault. Everything we do — that you do — *is* important, but we need to focus on *something*, do it well, and stop this frantic lifestyle."

The pain medication boggled her thought pattern. "God gave his Son's life for me. I think he got cheated." Her voice seemed to come from far off — a Vicodin tunnel.

He chuckled. "Honey, what are we trying to prove? Why do we live anxious, driven lives when all we are called to do is take his yoke and lean on him? We are his children. We have nothing to prove and certainly nothing to gain in this world."

"But he commands us to serve him and others."

"And what better service than being good stewards of what he has placed in our hands — our children, our finances, our relationship, our steadfast commitment to his grace. We need to decide who we can encourage with a phone call, a note, a good laugh, or a word of comfort. Those are the 'meetings' that will make a difference in this world."

She allowed the wisdom to wash over her. He was right, of course. They had nothing to prove: the cross had proved it all. He patted her, whispering, "Rest. I'll look after our family."

She reached out and blindly caught his hand, a hand that had loved and unselfishly protected her for twenty years. Her service to God was founded in respect, fidelity, and love. Her Lord asked for nothing more, nothing less. Why did she, and others, want to hang a price tag on God's grace? "I love you, Joey."

"I love you back, Rose." She listened to his soft footfall cross the room. Then the bedroom door quietly closed.

Jesus preached a simple religion. Man had complicated it and Rose abetted it.

A soft knock sounded.

"Yes?"

Anna poked her head through the open doorway. "Is it all right if I call Nick?"

"No!"

The door slammed.

Rose lay back wondering why the same God who preached patience in all things had thought up teenagers.

11
chapter

Rose woke with a start, confused. Where was she? Fragrant smells drifted from the kitchen. She could hear voices beyond the closed bedroom door. She stiffened. The family. She struggled to sit up, then quickly dropped back to the pillow.

A tap, followed by the door cracking open, and her sister-in-law, Jo, peered in. "Awake? We're about ready to eat. I thought you might need some help."

Rose tried to clear her foggy brain. "Help in doing what?"

"Getting ready to eat. It's the family dinner. That medicine's knocked you for a loop!"

Food? Eat? She couldn't cook! She couldn't think!

Jo crossed the room and sat down on the side of the bed. "Listen, I'm sorry I refused to have the dinner. It was very selfish of me, and next year I'm having it, no excuses."

Rose struggled to sit up, but it was impossible with Jo in the way. "You all came anyway?"

"Miss Christmas Eve? Not on your life! Joey called and pretty much laid down the law. He told us to get over here and get busy helping Anna cook." She grinned. "From the way he snapped out orders, we didn't dare disobey. Even Charlene showed up wearing an apron."

"I didn't know Charlene owned one."

"Must have been a joke shower gift. I'm sure she didn't go out and buy one for the occasion." Jo suddenly paused, forehead wrinkled in a frown. "But then again, recalling Joey's tone, maybe she did."

"He shouldn't have done that." Rose suppressed a grin. "Is Jamie here too?"

"Present and accounted for. She's the one who showed Anna how to cook the turkey, and she's peeled enough potatoes to feed half the town. Joey evidently put the fear in her. Charlene's enjoying herself so much, she asked what cookbook I'd recommend. She thinks she'd like to learn how to bake a cake."

Rose laughed outright. "Hand me my robe. I have to see this."

She entered the living room to find all of her family waiting. Mom and Dad sat on the sofa, holding court with their grandchildren, except for Anna who was bustling around the kitchen as if she had been cooking all her life. Her daughter paused to say something to Charlene, which set them both off in a fit of giggles.

The men had gathered around the TV in the den to watch a football game, stuffing themselves with sirupsnipper, and there, looking way too much at home, sat Nick Chalmers. And after she had told Anna she couldn't invite him. She would have a talk with that young lady later.

Rose snatched a cookie out of Eric's hand. "You're spoiling your dinner."

Someone got a touchdown. She didn't have a clue who was playing, but judging from the whoops from the men, it was the favored team. Joey high-fived Nick, then turned to do the same with Eric. Rose heaved a frustrated sigh. Men! They could bond over the silliest things, and it looked as if Joey liked the Chalmers boy.

Jamie slid her arm around Rose's waist. "He's a nice kid. Don't worry so much."

Rose leaned against her, welcoming this moment of sisterly closeness. "She's not your daughter."

"She's not," Jamie agreed. "But take time to get acquainted with Nick before you jump the gun. Remember it's not a perfect world, never will be."

Jo appeared in the doorway of the dining room. "Dinner is served."

Joey seated Rose and her eyes moved around the table, drinking in the sight of loved ones. Her family. She loved them all, and still she got aggravated at them sometimes. Did God get aggravated at his family too? For sure.

After her father asked the blessing, Joey carved the turkey, handing out slices of white and dark meat on request. Bowls of potatoes, gravy, green beans, cranberry salad, and an overwhelming array of food passed around the table. There was even lutefisk—the traditional Scandinavian fish dish. She glanced at her sister and sister-in-law, seated on either side of her.

"All right, who did this?"

Jamie grinned. "We did. Do you think you're the only one who can carry on the tradition?" She flashed a grin and leaned to hug Rose. "I can make sirupsnipper and lutefisk if I must, but I'll balk when it comes to providing seven different kinds of traditional cookies for the Christmas Eve table."

"You faker!" Rose grinned. "You know how to bake cookies!"

"But I don't want to bake cookies."

"But you must," Rose teased. "Next year, you and Jo will have the dinner."

Her sister frowned "Let's not get crazy."

A round of laughter broke out and the meal began.

After dishes were cleared, Rose's father took out the family Bible and read the Christmas story, the way he had done for as long as she could remember. Then it was time to leave for the Christmas Eve service.

Joey stood by her chair. "Are you sure you feel like going? If you don't, I'll stay home with you."

She smiled up at him. "That sounds tempting, but I think I'd like to go. Let me get dressed. I'm a little woozy, but I'll lean on you."

He bent and kissed her. "You can always lean on me."

Rose watched the comfortable bustle of family members donning coats and heavy gloves. The dinner had been excellent, the atmosphere relaxed and convivial, everyone appeared to have had a good time. Even Nick had seemed to enjoy himself. He'd fit in better than she expected. Jamie's words came back to her. *Give him a chance.* Well, maybe she would. In another five years, three years' difference in age wouldn't be so bad.

She watched him help Anna with her coat and take her arm as they walked to his pickup. Her little girl riding in that thing? *God, protect them.*

Joey helped her into the van. "Relax. They're only going to church."

"Right, relax." Not something she did all that well.

During the drive, Rose looked forward to the coming service, one of her favorite times of the Christmas celebration. When the family filed into the pews, the sanctuary glowed with greenery, poinsettias, and candlelight. The pastors were resplendent in white cassock robes and stoles the color of the Christmas season.

Rose said a prayer of thanksgiving, her family was all together, and they were healthy and happy. Blessed. So very blessed.

The sanctuary filled with people of all walks of life, come to celebrate their Savior's birth. The pipe organ swelled and the processional commenced with the cross, carried by a lay assistant, a banner, the robed choir, and the remaining clergy.

Rose relaxed, absorbing the familiar ritual. A sense of peace filled her as voices rose in praise.

Joey reached over and took her good hand, his fingers curling around hers. A warmth filled her. Joey, her children, her family—they were all so precious to her. How could she have so busied herself with committees and meetings that she had no time for them? For that was exactly what she had done. Joey had tried to tell her, but she hadn't understood. Here, in this holy place, set aside for worship of the Most High, she could see only too well how she had failed. Oh, she'd helped a few people, but she'd been too rushed to do a good job of anything.

Be still, and know that I am God.

The command echoed in her mind, as if God had singled her out. How could she truly worship God when she was too busy to be still and listen?

"Silent night," the choir sang. "Holy night."

It was indeed a holy night, the time set aside to celebrate the most precious gift given to mankind—Jesus, Savior of the world.

A blonde-haired young woman stepped forward to sing her solo. "All ... he wants ... is you."

Rose silently filled in the blanks. *Nothing else will do.* How could she have been so blind? God never required her to run herself ragged trying to serve him. She had chosen to fill her days and nights with self-appointed tasks someone else could have done as well, or better. She'd neglected her family, not in serving God, but in serving a twisted parody of his Word that benefited few. Instead of giving herself to God, she had tried to give him a laundry list of works.

She closed her eyes, reaching out in the only way she knew—through prayer. *I'm sorry, God. So sorry. I'll learn, and I'll do better. From now on, you direct my steps. Show me what's important and what's not.*

If all God wanted was this frustrated, harried, foolish woman, then she was ready to give herself over to him. Peace—sweet, comforting, overwhelming—flooded her. Tears stung her eyes, and her heart overflowed with love. Love for God, for Joey and her children, for her family gathered around her, for Blyth, Sue, and Jean. Love. That's what it was all about. Loving and giving through love. God had given her another chance, and this time she'd get it right.

After services, they emerged from church to see falling snow, like big tufts of cotton. Laughter broke out, hands reaching to catch pristine flakes. The family gathered back at Rose and Joey's. Hand in hand, they walked around the Christmas tree singing carols.

Afterwards, they gathered around the table for cookies and coffee, then on to the gift exchange. Rose loved to watch the look on her parents' faces when the family practiced the old customs.

Soon the living room was awash with wrapping paper, but this time Anna and Nick pitched in and cleaned up the mess.

Rose soaked in the festivities in a medicated bliss, thinking this had been the best Christmas Eve ever.

Even if she'd had to sprain a wrist in order to slow down.

An hour later, they said their last good-nights and Joey closed and locked the door. Sighing, Rose laid her head on her husband's shoulder. "It was a good Christmas Eve." He agreed that it was. A wonderful one. God was in control, not only in Rose's own life, but in Anna and Nick's. Rose just had to learn to trust.

"Honey," she kissed him. "Thank you for all your work, for making this one of the most memorable Christmases."

"It's great to be able to do something for you, Rose. I enjoyed it."

Later when they were in bed, Joey carefully put his arms around her, and she snuggled close.

"I hope the service wasn't too much for you."

"It wasn't," she assured him. "It was exactly what I needed."

Wait until he had a chance to get acquainted with the new Rose. The day after tomorrow she would go over her list of committees and cut it in half. In a few months, she'd halve the list again. Eric and Anna would find their mother available when they came home from school. Joey would have his wife back, and she'd cook a pot roast every night if he wanted it.

Joey gave a light snore.

Grinning, Rose let the medicine relax her. "Goodnight, Lord, and thank you for my best Christmas Eve yet."

advent

The word *advent* means "coming" or "arrival." The focus of the entire season is the celebration of the birth of Jesus Christ in his first advent, and the anticipation of the return of Christ the King in his second advent. Advent symbolizes the spiritual journey of individuals and a congregation, as they affirm that Christ has come, that he is present in the world today, and that he will come again in power.

12

chapter

Rose shifted, trying to find a position that didn't hurt. If it wasn't her back, it was a skinned knee, or a bruised elbow, or her little finger that throbbed in tandem with her heartbeat. Her sprained wrist ached every time she moved it. She hadn't known so many places could hurt. Her neck was stiff and sore, and her head felt like it was gripped in a vise. God had a way of slowing you down, invited or uninvited.

She rolled to her side, wide awake, incapable of finding relief, thinking it must be somewhere close to midnight. She wanted to ask for more medication, but she knew she had already had her four-hour quota. Joey stirred, and she felt a hand massaging her aching shoulders. Almost immediately, she started to relax, drifting into a medicated haze. She should feel guilty about disturbing him, but it was so comforting to have him beside her. This big, lovable Swede blessed her life in countless ways.

"Hurting, hon?"

113

"Humm." Tense muscles ached and her head pounded. "Joey?"

"Yeah?"

"I'm sorry about tonight. You were wonderful, but everything got dumped on you."

"Rose." She heard a teasing note in his tone. "It's the medicine talking, honey. Everything was great, and Charlene actually learned how to make gravy."

She giggled—well, a drug-induced snicker, actually. She had to admit the dinner went well. The family had survived. Next year Jo would have the dinner and she would help.

Joey rolled on his side to face her. "The family enjoyed the evening, even your mother."

"She did, didn't she? Yet I feel I let the family down this year."

He tenderly pulled her close, lightly touching his lips to the top of her hair. "You're the evening star of all our lives—you know that, don't you?"

She nodded, fighting back tears.

They lay holding each other, sharing the physical and spiritual intimacy that God grants a man and wife, two made as one, listening to the wind rattle the roof shingles. Rose finally broached the subject uppermost in her mind, trying to ease into the topic gently.

"What did you think of Nick Chalmers?"

"Good kid. Well mannered. Your mother liked him. Nick sat next to her at dinner and encouraged her to talk about Christmas when she was a girl. She actually mellowed toward the end—even had a few interesting stories."

"I missed that. Jo and Jamie were keeping me occupied at my end of the table. Did she tell any new stories?"

"No, only new versions."

Rose's thoughts returned to Nick and Anna. Her daughter had pulled a fast one, inviting him to dinner after she had been told in no uncertain terms not to invite him. No matter how charming Nick Chalmers was, she didn't trust a boy who wore a ponytail, an earring, and ripped jeans that hung below the waist. He was entirely too brash, overconfident, and had too many raging hormones to suit her. She still didn't want this near-man dating her daughter. Why couldn't Anna settle for someone more like her father—sweet, kind, generous, with short, neatly cropped hair?

A memory of Joey at Nick's age surfaced. He'd been bad in his own right, and she'd fallen hard. Had her mother felt the same uncertainty, this rash of worry when her daughter had fallen for the bold, outspoken kid she'd met at church?

Of course, the circumstances had been entirely different. She had been mature for her age. Anna was still a child.

"The kid's okay," Joey said. "Give him a chance."

"Have you seen his pickup?"

"Pickup, honey? That's not a 'pickup,' that's a sweet machine! The kid has initiative. He told me tonight that he worked summers for a car, had twenty-five hundred saved when he heard about an Internet site where you bid on government vehicles. He picked up an '86 one-ton Chevy 4x4 with a Dana 60 front axle and a TH400 automatic transmission for under twenty-five hundred. Can you believe that?"

"Dana 60 front axle, huh?" She had no inkling what he was talking about.

"Yeah, Nick gave me the website where he found it."

"Don't get any nutty ideas. We're not buying one."

He kissed her again. "You'd look good tooling around in a Hummer."

"As long as you're talking about birds, we're fine. If you're talking about those army tanks, forget it."

Chuckling, he gently massaged her back. "You won't find a Hummer on the site, but you never know what you might pick up. I'm going to check it out."

She realized this was the most time they'd spent talking in months. The nearness was nice, special.

Joey switched subjects. "Charlene seems like a nice kid."

"Our sister-in-law is not a kid. She's twenty-three and a married woman. It's time she settled down and had her share of family dinners."

"I think Eddy likes her exactly the way she is."

"Of course he does. He's too young to know better."

"Too much in love," Joey corrected. "The way we used to be."

"Used to be?" She stirred. "I thought we still were."

"We are, but not that crazy, wild, impetuous love." Joey rubbed the knotted tendons in her neck. "We're older now, more experienced."

She half-rose on her elbow. "You mean you're no longer in love with me?"

"Of course I am, but it's different." He eased her back on the bed. "We know each other now. Like the Bible says, the two of us have become one. Eddy and Charlene are still building their relationship. Young love is great, exciting, and wears you out. Mature love is the best kind. Comfortable, yet the love keeps growing. Eddy and Charlene don't share what we have, but they will someday."

Rose snuggled closer to his warmth. "I so love you, Joey."

"You'd better." He kissed her. "And now if you're feeling better, I need to get a couple hours of sleep. Santa comes tonight, you know. Ho, ho, ho."

"Eric and Anna don't expect ... "

He laid a finger across his lips. "I pray to God that none of us ever stops expecting. Ever stops dreaming. That we all remain childlike and hopeful in our expectations. I believe that pleases God the most."

"Amen," she whispered. She needed to pray that on this most sacred of nights, the celebration of the Savior's birth would be realized.

She eased closer so she could look up at him in the darkness. On impulse, she reached up to hook one arm around his neck, pulling his head down slowly to meet hers. His lips were warm and seeking, and she knew he was hers. Like the Bible said, they were joined together forever. She wanted Anna to experience the same all-consuming love.

"Merry Christmas, Joey."

Joey's lips brushed her hair. "Don't worry so much about Nick and Anna. God has our daughter's life in hand."

A moment later he rolled to his side, and shortly afterwards she heard his breathing become slow and even. She muffled a whimper as she carefully shifted to her back.

A thin glow of streetlight filtered through the lacy curtain, throwing deep shadows into the remote corners. This was the only Christmas since she had been married and had children that she hadn't been in a panicked state, racing around, trying to do a dozen things at once. *Be still, and know that I am God.* The Bible verse had never held more meaning. Rarely was she still long enough to know that God was God, to rest in his assurance.

The pain eased enough for Rose to drop off to sleep. At first, she tumbled into deep slumber, almost exhausting in its intensity, but gradually faces and forms took shape. She heard voices. Familiar faces danced through the drug-enhanced sleep, flitting in and out with no obvious purpose, jolting her awake. She tried to orient her thoughts. She was in bed with Joey sleeping beside her. The house had a predawn feel about it. Why was her sleep haunted by barely perceived forms, like something out of her past? Must be the Vicodin.

Her eyelids were so heavy she couldn't hold them open. Gradually they drifted shut, ushering in more faces. She was running down the highway carrying a paper bag containing a Big Mac and fries covered in horseradish.

She had no idea what that represented.

"Horseradish clears the sinuses," she heard Joey say.

"Hmm?" She stirred. "Who said that?" Rose mumbled the words, but no one answered. The highway was long and dark, broken by the glow of car lights that approached and flashed by. She had to find a place to stop and eat. Instead she continued running down the highway wearing rubber thongs, carrying the bag with the Big Mac and fries.

Got to gain weight, got to gain weight. Too thin, too thin! The words beat out the cadence like jungle drums.

She woke confused, drenched in sweat. What had that been all about?

Big Mac. She eased the blankets aside. Joey stirred.

Sleep reclaimed her, only to release her thirty minutes later, according to the lighted numbers of her bedside clock. Would this night ever end? The mantel clock chimed the half hour. Three-thirty and no one was stirring. Not even a mouse.

Trapped in a semiconscious solitude, she stared at the ceiling, allowing her mind to drift over Joey's concerns about her busy life and the past hectic month. When had she gotten on this treadmill? It had started gradually, slipping up on her—busy, busy, busy.

She stirred when images of Jean standing in the church service and sharing her fears about Ken flashed through her mind. Had Rose really been so busy that she couldn't have stopped, taken the young woman in her arms, and cried with her? Prayed with her—maybe not out loud, but silently, together?

And Sue, the hypochondriac. All she sought was a word of assurance, but Rose had been so busy she hadn't picked up the phone to learn that Sue had discovered a lump in her breast. That was not manufactured fear—that was every woman's nightmare.

Recurring flashbacks tripped through her mind as shadowy apparitions. Blyth. Her son was on drugs, a serious problem, but not critical to one whose son never gave her a moment's problem until the smoking incident.

Joey's voice. *"Smoking in the bathroom, Rose! Maybe he knows his parents are too busy to talk when he needs guidance!"*

Rose reached out to lightly touch Joey, sleeping beside her. In the twenty years of their married life, she had never had reason to doubt his love and fidelity. How many women could make that claim?

She held her breath. Smoke? Had she smelled smoke?

No. The fireplace—she smelled the fireplace. Her stomach churned with medication and too much of the Christmas turkey she'd consumed. Should have had Joey bring her an antacid the last time he'd been up to get her medication. She'd wake him now—no, he needed his sleep. Her eyelids fluttered. Need to wake up.

She woke with a start, and then drifted.

Blyth. Hollow-eyed, shaken, Blyth, struggling to deal with her husband's death and a son who had turned to drugs. She'd given compassion that morning with an eye on the clock. After all, Eric had been exemplary due to what? Her and Joey's expert parenting skills?

Through God's grace, Eric had yet to experiment with drugs, but he could. He could. And where and to whom would she turn for solace? God, yes, certainly. Friends? She prayed there would be a few who would rise to the occasion. A child on drugs didn't always work out for the best. Sometimes it didn't work out at all.

"Have faith and everything will be fine." So where was the Scripture reference for that? The disciples had faith and they had become martyrs. Faith was not an insurance policy against pain. Missionaries who had given their life in a foreign land knew that God did not grant promises on demand.

"You just need to trust God more." She shuddered, rolling to her side. Tears trickled from the corners of her eyes. Who made her an expert on trust?

God, forgive me. Help me to rethink my purpose, to serve you in a way that will make you proud.

advent

The Advent candles' light itself becomes an important symbol for the season. The light reminds us that Jesus is the light of the world, which comes into the darkness of our lives to bring newness, life, and hope. It also reminds us that we are called to be a light to the world as we reflect the light of God's grace to others.

13
chapter

Watery rays of dawn leaked through the curtain. Rose stirred, thankful the long night was over. Christmas Day. The Lord's birthday. All over the world bright-eyed children clambered out of bed and scampered for the tree, while others knelt in predawn church services to offer humble gratitude.

She watched the pale square of light spread across the carpet, gray dawn gradually illuminating the room. How had she lost sight of such simplicity? God never meant for his Word to be so complicated. Man had added rituals and regulations, often stifling the joy of Christian living. She needed change. She needed to take a close look at Christ's life and see if she could find one single casserole or bundt cake. Bundt cakes and casseroles were fine when one was physically hungry, but the spiritually needy wanted more, deserved more.

She thought of the woman who had crept through the crowd, and with amazing faith, reached out and brushed the hem of Jesus's robe. And her faith healed her.

Rose had faith, but for the first time, she realized she did not accurately understand what Christ meant when he commanded, "Love one another." Truly love one another.

With God's help she could change. She would change. Starting today, this day of renewed hope.

She nudged Joey, trying to wake him so she could share her newfound knowledge. "Joey? Honey?" He mumbled something indistinguishable. "Joey?" she whispered in his ear, wanting to wake him gently.

"Huh?" He gradually opened his eyes and then sat upright. "What? More Vicodin?" He threw back the sheet and his bare feet hit the floor. Rose reached out a restraining hand. She pulled lightly at his shoulder and he folded back into bed, yanking the sheet over his head. He was back asleep in moments.

Rose sighed, easing closer to his warmth. The medicine was working its magic; nothing hurt. Joey rolled over facing the wall. Rose glanced his way and scooted closer. Wrapping her arms around his waist, she whispered, "The moment I'm back on my feet, I am going to have lunch with Jean. Three hours, maybe longer. I'll let her talk — that's all she wants. Someone to listen. I don't have to have an answer, but I can listen."

"Umm?"

"Nothing, darling, go back to sleep."

She began to pray, relishing her time with the Father. It had been too long since they'd talked, one of those Father-daughter talks. She had plenty of time. No hurry. No rush. For once, Rose Bergmen was in no hurry.

She had all the time he allotted her.

Standing under a hot shower, Rose relished the driving water needles massaging her sore muscles. She was so stiff she thought she might have to call for assistance to get dressed, but a clean robe sufficed. Anna was already in the kitchen looking helpless, but apparently eager to help in a crisis. Rose came in and sat down at the table. "Merry Christmas, honey. If you'll bring me a pillow, I'll help you cook breakfast."

"Merry Christmas, Mom." Anna smiled. "I know how to do scrambled eggs, but that's about it. Where's Dad?"

"Still sleeping."

Anna brought a pillow, carefully inserting it between Rose's back and the chair. "What do I do first?"

Rose leaned back, feeling much better than expected. The fog was still there, but lifting. "First of all, make coffee. Your father can't wake up without it."

"Coffee." Anna got the beans and poured them into the grinder. Soon the rich aroma of Colombian roast filled the early morning air.

"Now," Rose said, "we have croissants from the bakery. Get the heavy skillet. Add butter. Break a dozen eggs into a bowl, and in a second skillet, fry sausage. We'll have breakfast sandwiches."

"Gotcha." Anna got the sausage patties from the freezer and slapped them in the cold cast-iron skillet as if she had been doing it all her life. She adjusted the burner heat, and then took eggs from the refrigerator, breaking them carefully into the blue pottery bowl.

Rose heard the shower running. One of the men in the family was up. Joey joined them shortly, his hair still wet. That left Eric. Like most thirteen-year-olds, he would have to be dragged from bed.

Ten minutes later, her son entered the kitchen, surprising her. She grinned. "You're up early."

"Thought I'd better get up and supervise the cooking. After all, if I have to eat it, I want to be sure it's done right."

A short time later, the family gathered around the table, holding hands for the blessing. Joey thanked God for the day. Rose blinked back tears when she heard him thank the Father for each family member, expressing how much each person meant to him and asking his special favor on them. He requested healing for Rose and wisdom for Eric and Anna.

After the echoed amens, Anna set the platter of sandwiches on the table, beaming with pride. "Eat hearty. I know they're good. I made them myself."

Eric lifted the top half of the croissant, peering suspiciously at the ingredients. "Promise this won't make me sick?"

"I promise if you don't eat every bite of it, I'll tell your friends you used my sweet violet shower gel."

He glowered at his sister. "That's blackmail."

"You got it." She grinned. "Want seconds?"

Rose met Joey's eyes and smiled. How long had it been since they had laughed together, prayed as a family? Far, far too long.

Even before they delved into the Christmas stockings, she knew this moment was the best gift of all.

After, Joey and Eric cleaned up the wrappings from the last gifts, they dropped onto the sofa to watch football. Rose remained in the kitchen with Anna.

"We'll make soup for lunch. Get out the Crock-pot, the big one," she instructed. "We're going to make baked potato soup. Use the kitchen shears to cut the bacon into small pieces and put it in the cast-iron skillet. Let it cook while you chop the onions and potatoes, and then add them to the broth."

Anna started on the bacon. "This is fun. We ought to do it more often. I've always wanted to know how to cook. Can you teach me to make lutefisk and lefse and sirupsnipper?"

"You really want to know?"

"I want our traditions to never change."

"Anna ... I didn't know ... "

Her daughter frowned. "Well, you were always so busy, I didn't want to bother you."

Rose swallowed the lump in her throat.

"You're never a bother to me. I know I've been too busy, but that's going to change. From now on I'm going to spend more time with my family and less time with busy stuff." She couldn't give up all her busywork, but she could prioritize.

"Really?" Anna ceased cutting bacon to look at her. "You mean that?"

"I mean it. I'm going to be underfoot so much, you'll be longing for the good old days."

"Not a chance." Her daughter dumped the bacon into the skillet and started on the onions. When the bacon was crispy, she stirred it into the broth mixture and poured it into the Crock-pot.

"Now cut up the cheese," Rose instructed. "Add it to the soup mixture."

"The whole box? That's a lot of cheese."

"The whole two pounds. Add it to the hot soup mixture and let it melt."

Anna looked up while cutting cheese.

"Mom, is it all right if Nick comes over this afternoon? We wanted to listen to his new iPod and hang out."

Rose caught her breath. Anna's expression turned expectant, waiting for her mother's reaction. After hesitating a second too long, Rose nodded. "Sure, that would be fine."

"You don't really like him, do you?"

Rose sighed. "I know you're growing up, but I'm not ready for you to get serious about anyone yet."

"Well, Mom. Serious happens."

"Yeah, it does. That's what I'm afraid of."

Anna laughed, and Rose glanced up, surprised. "Mom. I know what you're worried about, but Nick's a solid guy. He may look a little rough around the edges, but he's strong in his faith and so am I. We both plan to go on to college and finish our education. If it works out between us, fine. If it doesn't, well, that's fine too, but either way, we enjoy each other's company right now. That's all it amounts to. If the situation changes, I'll let you know."

It was that situation changing that worried Rose. If Nick had been a little less Nick, it would have helped. She bit her lip and looked up to meet her daughter's eyes. "You grew up too fast. You changed from a little girl to a young woman while I wasn't looking."

She had just put her finger on the problem. She hadn't been looking. While she was running the town, taking care of everyone else, her children had grown up.

IRELAND
Nollaig Shona Duit

On Christmas Eve, in honor of the infant Jesus, the youngest family member is chosen to light a candle in the window. The light is a welcome to any who, like Mary and Joseph, might be looking for shelter. The candle burns all night long, and wanderers who pass by are given food and money. After church services on Christmas Day, families distribute baked goods to friends and relatives. The season ends on January 6, which is known as "Little Christmas."

advent

On New Year's Eve, Rose and Joey sat in the kitchen nook alone. In a little while, Eric and Anna were going to the youth Watch party at the church. Nick was driving them, and if he minded having Eric tag along, he was hiding it well. The three were in the living room now singing tunes a tad off key. Nick had brought his guitar and seemed to be encouraging Eric to learn how to play. Their laughter filled the house.

Joey grinned. "I don't think they're ready for *American Idol*, do you?"

Rose shook her head. "They're loud—does that count?"

"Giving it all they've got." He lifted his coffee cup. "I think they're planning to debut tonight at the Watch party."

Rose moved her cup a few inches to the left, brushing away imaginary crumbs. "You don't mind staying home tonight?"

"Get real. I love it! We can turn on the television and have a quiet Watch party of our own. Pop some corn, play some old CDs."

Clearing her throat, she looked up. "I wanted to talk to you about that. Would you care if I went out?"

Surprise flashed across his features. "Without me? You're not completely healed yet. It's too soon for you to resume normal activities."

"I don't intend to ever resume 'normal' activities," she assured him. "I told you about Blyth's son, the one on drugs."

"Yes?"

"She sits home alone and waits for him. Tonight's going to be tough. She's bound to be more worried than usual. I thought I'd go sit with her until Frank comes home."

Joey was silent for a minute, and then he smiled. "You know, I don't think I'd mind staying home alone. You go be with Blyth. We have the rest of our lives together, and I think she needs you tonight."

Rose eased out of the chair and walked around the table to sit on his lap. She draped her arms around his neck. "You know, I really do love you."

"I know. It's because I'm so darn lovable." She snickered.

His arms closed around her and they kissed. They were alone in the world for a moment. A very short moment.

"Hey, you guys, cut out the mush!" Rose opened her eyes to see Eric leaning against the kitchen doorframe. "Can't we leave you two alone for a minute?"

Nick and Anna hovered behind him, grinning. Joey tightened his arms around Rose. "Go back to your music. If we need you, we'll call."

The kids laughed and disappeared to the living room. Joey rested his cheek against hers.

"We've got a lot to be thankful for, Mrs. Bergmen."

"God's been good. Better than we deserve."

And from now on, she was going to take better care of what he had given her.

Later, Rose hobbled up Blyth's porch steps. Christmas tree lights spilled from the window to the porch floor. A wreath hung on the door. She reached out and caught a snowflake blown into the shelter of the porch. Opening her gloved hand, she examined the tiny creation, different from any other flake. For the first time ever, she felt like she was looking upon the face of God.

Closing her eyes, she shivered, experiencing the true Christmas spirit—a week late, but no less awesome. She pressed the doorbell.

Blyth opened the door almost immediately, curiosity coloring her dark eyes. Rose understood her surprise. They really didn't know each other that well, just worked at the thrift store together on alternate weeks. Worry lines etched Blyth's face."

"Rose? Goodness, should you be out in this weather ... and so soon after your fall?" She held the door against the swirling snow.

"I'm okay, just stiff and sore." She lifted her bandaged wrist. "I have plenty of aspirin. It'll do me good to get out for a while."

Blyth stepped aside, allowing her entrance to the foyer. She appeared to hold back, her eyes questioning why Rose was there. They had never visited in each other's homes.

Rose unwound her scarf, welcoming the house's warmth. "I thought I'd sit with you tonight until your son gets home."

Blyth's mouth dropped open, her eyes widened, and then her features crumpled as tears welled to her eyes. She stepped into Rose's waiting arms. "Thank you ... thank you so very much."

"My pleasure," Rose murmured, holding her tightly.

Tonight really was the start of a new beginning, the start of a ministry that could change the world, or at least change Rose's part of the world. She took a deep breath, silently echoing Blyth's thoughts. *Thank you, Father, thank you so very much.*

AUTHOR'S NOTE

God never ceases to amaze me. While I was writing this novella, I received an email from a close writing friend, Hannah Alexander. She had received the following letter, and she thought it was so profound in its simplicity, so beautiful, that she wanted to share it. While the subject concerns situations a writer faces, the concept is the same in our personal lives.

Every word expressed in this note is the very essence of what I hoped to convey in *Unwrapping Christmas*. The author of the note, Karen Hancock, said it so much more eloquently. I feel that God sent the letter to help me convey the message.

I approached Karen with the idea of including her letter at the end of my story, and she graciously agreed. My Christmas prayer is that Karen's words will bless and minister to you, enrich your life, and boost your spiritual walk, as much as they have mine.

Merry Christmas!

Lori Copeland

JESUS DIDN'T HURRY

Karen Hancock

Jesus was never in a hurry. He accomplished the greatest work a man ever accomplished in only three and a half years, yet he was never worried or hurried or flustered or stressed. He wasn't concerned with building a big ministry, either, nor was he rushing off to do this or that, urging his disciples to get this or that, going to see such and such. He stopped and talked to the people who came into his life without checking his watch. His disciples did not stand at his elbow reminding him he had to be in Capernaum by sundown or Jerusalem by the next day. Sometimes he just went fishing.

The thing that struck me was that sometimes it's okay to do nothing. Because this concept is bound up in what I am learning about the creative process, I find this especially exciting. After a cell is finished dividing there is a period of rest before anything else happens. If cell division is about growth, and it is, then growth is about rest. This seems an obvious fact when you look at children, who grow at prodigious rates and yet need a lot of rest. Even as adults God has created us to require about eight hours of sleep every night. Americans seem on a headlong charge to do away with rest and sleep as quickly as possible.

Article after article documents the growing epidemic of sleep deprivation and everyone is always in a hurry, always pressed for time despite the time savers of fast food, fast cars, and a fast Internet. With cell phones, microwaves, and bagged, ready-to-eat lettuce, we have more time than ever and yet seem more frazzled than ever. Voices from our media-saturated lives constantly offer us new things to do and have, new ways to achieve, new areas to improve so we can get more done. There isn't much talk about doing nothing. Whatever happened to "come unto me, all you who are weary and heavy laden, and I will give you rest?" As believers we are children fully accepted by our Father already. Why do we need to do all these things? What are we trying to prove?

I count it no accident that the Father called Jesus his beloved son in whom he was well pleased before he had done one thing in his ministry. The Bible's silence on those years between ages twelve and thirty is also not an accident. He wasn't doing great things for God during those times. And God made it a point to declare him already beloved and well-pleasing anyway. As believers, we are in union with him and thus we too are beloved and well-pleasing before we do anything.

So why are we so obsessed with achieving things? Why must we live harried, driven lives when all we are called to do is take his yoke and learn of him? As children of God, we have nothing to prove and nothing in this world to gain. Seek him first and all things will be added to your life, Matthew tells us. David wrote of grace and mercy pursuing him, not the other way around.

Jesus was not in a hurry. I don't have to be either. I don't have to worry about meeting my deadline, because he will see to that. I don't have to worry about building a big ministry, because he will see it is whatever size he has chosen it to be. I don't have anything to prove because children of God don't have to prove anything. I only have to follow him and learn of him, and in so doing, I will find the rest that is the Christian way of life.

> "Come to me, all you who are weary and burdened, and I will give you rest. Take my yoke upon you and learn from me, for I am gentle and humble in heart, and you will find rest for your souls. For my yoke is easy and my burden is light."
> Matthew 11:28–30

ENJOY THE BERGMENS' HOLIDAY TRADITIONS

Lutefisk Swedish Christmas Codfish

3 pounds codfish

salt

mustard sauce:

    1½ cups beef stock

    1 tablespoon dry brown mustard

    1 tablespoon vinegar

    1 teaspoon sugar

    1 teaspoon cornstarch

    ½ teaspoon salt

    ¼ teaspoon white pepper

    ¼ teaspoon paprika

Wash and skin fish, cut into several large pieces. Place the pieces close together on a square of cheesecloth and sprinkle with salt; wrap loosely and place on a rack in a large kettle. Add water to cover and bring to a boil over moderate heat. Reduce heat and simmer for twenty minutes or until tender. Drain and arrange on a warm platter. Serve with melted butter or mustard sauce. Surround with little boiled potatoes and green peas.

Mustard sauce: Use wire whisk to combine all ingredients thoroughly. Heat to boiling, stirring constantly. As soon as the mixture is slightly thickened, strain and serve.

Potato Lefse

Lefse is a great Scandinavian treat, often described as the Queen Mother of Norwegian pastries. Ways to eat it are as varied as the recipes to be found. Some roll it with butter and sugar, some with baked pork, and some even eat it with hot dogs. True connoisseurs insist that lefse should be only made with fresh cooked potatoes, others say that lefse made with instant potatoes is just as good.

4 cups cooked potatoes (riced)

½ cup butter (no substitutes)

1½ cups flour

½ teaspoon salt

Boil potatoes in salted water. Rice the potatoes, blend in butter. Chill. Work in 1½ cups flour very well. Form this dough into small balls (1/3 cup), as if forming a bun, working in a small amount of flour. Roll thin on well-floured board. Fry on ungreased lefse iron at 475 degrees to 500 degrees until light brown spots appear, turn and fry other side a few moments.

Lefse hints:

Apply flour to rolling pin and pastry cloth. Roll dough until very thin. (If you have trouble picking the lefse up, roll it onto the turning stick, then roll it back off when you place it on the grill.)

Stack finished lefses between two cloth towels to cool. It is important to cool the lefses between towels to keep them from drying out. When complete, restack the lefses once or twice to remove some of the moisture to keep them from getting soggy.

Never use products containing grease on an aluminum-finish lefse grill if you want to use it for lefse again. The grease will destroy the seasoning that has built up on the grill and make it impossible to prevent the lefse from sticking. If you for some reason have a sticky spot on your grill, take a small piece of steel wool and go in a circular motion around the surface of the grill (following the original sanding marks). Once you feel you have the sticky spot removed, rub flour onto the surface of the grill, just like when it was new.

Dough is much easier to roll if still a bit chilled.

Potatoes should be done a day ahead and refrigerated. Dough must be rolled soon after mixing.

Sirupsnipper

9 tablespoons cream

½ cup + 2½ tablespoons corn syrup

½ cup + 2½ tablespoons sugar

7 tablespoons butter (no substitutes)

2 cups flour

¼ teaspoon pepper

¼ teaspoon ginger

¼ teaspoon anise

¼ teaspoon cinnamon

¾ teaspoon hartshorn salt

¾ teaspoon baking soda

almonds, blanched, for decorating

Boil cream, syrup, and sugar together. Stir in butter and let mixture cool until lukewarm. Sift in dry ingredients and knead the dough to mix thoroughly. Chill overnight. Roll dough out as thin as possible and cut into diamond shapes. Lay on a greased baking sheet. Place half a blanched almond on each cookie. For a shiny finish, brush cookies with egg white. Bake at 350 degrees F for five minutes.

Read a sample chapter from Lori Copeland's *Now and Always*. Coming in 2008!

1

Very few things distracted Katie Addison when she was on a mission, but the sight of three dead horses strewn across the highway stopped her in her tracks. The Jeep skidded and veered to the right before stopping. Passing motorists set out flares, and highway patrol began the process of diverting traffic around the gruesome sight. Putting a tissue over her nose, Katie exited the Jeep, hurrying to the scene. Thick smoke covered the area from the burning fire on the ridge below Devils Tower. Wildfire had broken out in the thirteen-hundred-acre park, and crews had been battling it all day. A suffocating haze blanketed the area.

Confusion reigned as Katie threaded her way through curious onlookers and fellow travelers who'd stopped to help. Her eyes focused on the black skid marks, and it didn't take a sleuth to see that the overturned truck and stock trailer had veered to the center and jackknifed, blocking most of the road.

Blowout? Deer standing in the road?

The long, white trailer lay on its side in the ditch. The sides were enclosed and the top was lined with openings for ventilation. The terrified screams from trapped horses, kicking and lunging, trying to break free, sent a shudder up her spine. She'd lived on a ranch all her life, and while she wasn't a vet, she knew almost as much as anybody about animals. She took care of her own — three dogs, three cats, a goat, and a lame Appaloosa, and she'd sewn up more than one wire cut by lantern light.

She approached a uniformed officer trying to redirect traffic. "Is the driver hurt?"

"Don't know, ma'am. An ambulance is on the way."

She strained to see beyond the man's imposing height. Men worked to free the truck's passenger-side door while others were trying to break into the mangled trailer. Katie watched for a few minutes, and then impulsively raced to help, her former mission forgotten.

Working her way around the overturned trailer, she tried to peer through the narrow slits in the side wall. It was impossible to count the heaving flesh trapped inside, but she estimated three, maybe four horses down, kicking and struggling to get out. Men worked feverishly to reach the injured animals, but the enclosed trailer defeated their efforts. The back door hung by one hinge, but the divider separating the back compartment from the front was jammed, making it almost impossible to reach the injured. Apparently the dead animals had been thrown out when the trailer jackknifed. Some had been hit by cars, judging from the damaged autos scattered along the roadside. A portly man collapsed against the overturned trailer, breathing heavily and wiping sweat from his forehead. The cloud of smoke cast a stifling blanket, hampering rescue efforts.

Katie crawled inside the overturned carrier, cautiously working her way to the crumpled and jammed divider. Her stomach curled at the sight of the tangled limbs of the horrified and injured horses. There had to be a way to get them out. A bay kicked frantically, lunging against the divider. Blood spurted from a nasty shoulder gash.

"There, boy, take it easy," Katie crooned, trying to calm the horse.

A shout and the wail of a siren heralded the arrival of emergency vehicles. Katie crawled through the wreckage and emerged as an ambulance, two fire trucks, and a couple of police cars pulled up, sirens blaring. Paramedics hit the ground before the vehicle fully stopped, racing to the truck cab. Firemen approached the overturned trailer, eyes openly assessing the bedlam. Katie wanted to scream at them to hurry, but she knew they needed to determine what would be best for the horses' sake. Someone brought a Sawzall. Was it strong enough to slice through the metal trailer? Rescue workers were already using the Jaws of Life to cut through the truck cab and reach the driver pinned inside.

The screech of metal cutting metal sent the horses into a panic. Firemen cut through the top of the trailer, and the minute it was open, Katie tried to maneuver into line to help remove the animals, but a burly captain stepped in front of her.

"Sorry, ma'am. You need to step back out of the way."

"I can help. I've doctored animals all my life."

"You could get hurt in there. Sorry, but if you want to help, you'll stand back and let us work."

A tall, rawboned woman with short salt-and-pepper hair ran toward them. "I'm a vet." She was allowed to pass to the scene of action, while Katie fumed. A couple of men cautiously approached the trailer. Katie held her breath as they tried to untangle the downed animals. Finally they led the bay out at the end of a rope. One by one, the horses were removed. Frightened, shying at every noise, the trembling animals were led to safety. Two were limping, and all were bleeding from numerous wounds. A stock trailer rattled up, restoring alarm. The men leading the horses spoke calmly, guiding them gently forward. One horse couldn't get up. "Broken legs and internal injuries," someone in the crowd murmured. The vet administered an injection, and after a short time, the thrashing body went limp and the horrible sound of an animal in agony was stilled. The carcass was dragged out and loaded onto a flatbed trailer.

The woman vet glanced at Katie, her color drained. "Those horses look like someone took a ball bat to them. It's a shame to allow this to happen in a civilized nation. Someone ought to do something about this disgrace." A fireman called her and she moved away to join him.

What disgrace? Accidents happen.

A news reporter held a microphone to the fire chief's mouth, and Katie shamelessly eavesdropped. "How many horses were saved?"

"Four. At first we thought we had four in the trailer, but when we got inside, one was down and buried under the weight of the others. Eight horses in all were involved."

"Are the remaining ones going to be all right?"

"Can't say." The chief lifted his hat for ventilation. "You'll need to talk to the vet — looked to me like most of them were hurt pretty badly. They got tossed around when the trailer overturned."

Attendants strapped the driver to a body board and loaded him into the ambulance. A stench of oil and spilled gas, of blood and sweat and death, hung over the scene of the accident like a thundercloud mingling with the sharp, stinging scent of smoke.

Devils Tower, the first vertical monolith to be named a national monument, loomed in the distance. The massive

rock formation jutted out of the smoky Black Hills land-
scape, looking almost surreal with the smoke billowing
around its base and the flickering flames skirting the ridge.
Katie knew several northern plains tribes called it Bear's
Lodge and considered it a sacred worship site. It was probably best known for the role it played in the late seventies
movie *Close Encounters*. Today, the tower, the smoke, the
tragic wreck, sent a shiver of apprehension rippling through
her. She breathed a quick prayer.

*Father, be with the driver, and with these helpless ani-
mals. You can work miracles, and it looks like the victims
could sure use one.*

"The driver will be lucky to get out of this alive."

Katie turned to find Joel Tate beside her. Joel owned
the ranch two miles to the south. Except for the seven
years he'd spent on Wall Street, he'd been a fixture in these
parts. They'd gone to school together, known each other
most of their lives. Joel had been back a few weeks, but this
was the first time she'd bumped into him.

"It's so tragic. Does anyone know how it happened?"

He inclined his head toward the distorted wreckage.
"The driver hasn't regained consciousness."

Katie's eyes scanned the highway where carcasses were
being loaded onto the flatbed trailer. "It's a miracle anything survived."

He lifted his Stetson and ran a hand through black,
curly hair. Katie had to admit the man just got better look-

ing with age. His odd colored eyes, a dark green hue, had been a distraction during his youth; now they enhanced his rugged features. In high school he'd been the bookish sort, not particularly handsome, and certainly not part of the "in crowd." He hadn't been a partier. She'd liked that about him, but others called him a geek. Well, world, Joel Tate was anything but a geek now. Katie thought he'd be married by now with a houseful of kids and an immense library. Thirty-seven wasn't ancient, but most men were committed by that age, yet Joel remained single.

He was a couple of inches taller than her own six feet, which made it nice standing beside him. It hadn't been easy in high school when she had towered above him and most boys her age.

Maybe he was like her, content to wait until the right person came along, though rumor had it, he'd been involved in a pretty nasty breakup prior to leaving the Big Apple.

She didn't have time to brood about her lack of social life. Taking care of Grandpops until he died took time, then working the shelter . . . She glanced at her watch. "Oh, granny's skirts! I was due at the airport fifteen minutes ago!"

Joel turned to look at her. "New guest?"

She nodded. Everyone around knew that she took in battered women, but the town kept the information to themselves. Little Bush was a close-knit community, loyal to a fault, and the Addisons had been part of the community as far back as anyone remembered. It wasn't a large community, though it had grown since she graduated from high school. For one thing, a couple of factories had moved in, and a few hometown boys made good, investing time and money into the community. Quite a few mom-and-pop businesses had sprung up, and the chamber of commerce boasted a healthy number of members. The town still had most of the original buildings, reminding one that it was an old town, it's roots going back a long way. There was still a hint of wildness, a feel of the frontier that outsiders sometimes found intimidating. If they wanted something more, Sundance and Gillette were a short drive away.

Katie's Grandpops, old man Addison, as the locals called him, ran the town before he died last year. Paul and Willa Addison, her maternal grandparents, had raised Katie from an infant when their daughter had been shot and killed by her jealous husband.

With abuse in her background, if mistreated women needed protection, Katie gave it and Little Bush enforced it. Her thoughts returned to Joel. "What happens to the surviving animals?" She stepped back to allow an emergency worker to pass.

He shook his head. "They were on their way to the slaughter house. I suppose they'll continue the journey."

Her jaw dropped. Slaughter house! She knew these things happened, but ... slaughter house?

"Why?"

"Why? Surely you know why."

Oh, she knew why, and she knew animal by-products were a huge business, but to see evidence of the cruelty turned Katie's stomach. Sure, she was accused of taking in every stray that wandered her way, and if her house and yard were any indication of being a pushover, she couldn't argue with the accusation, but horses, innocent animals, on their way to becoming glue or paste, or whatever they did with them?

"The survivors—I want them."

Joel glanced over. "You want them?"

"Yes. I want them. Who do I talk to?"

He shook his head, a grin shadowing the corners of his mouth. His clean shaven features hadn't changed much over the years; his youthful complexion had cleared but left some remaining evidence on his cheeks. Wall Street's pressure had done a job on him, folks said, made him cynical. Sick of life. He pretty much stayed to himself, only going into town for groceries and supplies every couple of weeks.

He shifted. "I see the years haven't changed you."

"Meaning what?"

"Meaning you're still trying to take care of the whole world."

She shrugged. "And that's a bad thing?" That was most people's problem; because they couldn't take care of everything, they quit trying to take care of the things they could. She believed one person's efforts, regardless of how puny, made a difference, and she tried to live her life accordingly.

Her cell phone rang and she punched the on button. "Yes, this is Katie. Oh ... hi. Yes, I meant to call you this morning about the feed bill. I'll have the payment to you by morning—yes, in the morning. No later, Sue." She flashed a lame grin in Joel's direction. "Yeah, can't really talk now. Thanks for calling." She clicked the off button and resumed the conversation without missing a beat. "I really have to go. Who do I see about getting the animals?"

"You've got room for four near dead horses?"

"I'll make room."

Shaking his head, he focused on the activity. "I haven't acquired injured horses on their way to the slaughter house, but I suppose if I were planning on it, I'd start by consulting Ben. Most likely he can trace the owner's name, maybe talk to the people at the USDA or humane society."

"Ben?" Her eyes traced the sheriff who was busy trying to redirect traffic. "You think he'd help?" Not likely. She and Ben had been at sword's point of late. She wasn't sure he would be overly eager to help her. Their on-and-off again dating over the years was starting to get on his nerves. Like Joel, she'd known Ben most of her life, and while it wasn't secret that he'd had a crush on her longer than anybody in Little Bush could remember, Katie didn't return the sentiment. He was great guy, but he was Ben. Kind, courteous, good-looking some would say, with reddish blond hair and tiger green eyes, but Ben was Ben. Familiar. Safe. Not what God had in mind for her mate.

"You'd have to pay the person who owns them something, I suppose — though if they're injured enough, he might pay you to take them off his hands."

Katie shrugged and scribbled down the information on a notepad. "Thanks Joel. Good to see you back."

Monday Morning Faith

Lori Copeland

Dear Mom and Pop,

Two days ago we all spent the afternoon in palm trees. One of the village dogs broke his leash and treed the whole community. The dog is mean, but I have managed to form a cautious relationship with him by feeding him scraps from our table, and jelly beans ... I hope candy doesn't hurt a dog; it hasn't hurt this dog, I can assure you.

I know you're wondering about Sam ... I love him with all my heart, but sometimes love isn't enough.

Love always,

Johanna

Librarian Johanna Holland likes her simple life in Saginaw, Michigan. So why is she standing in the middle of the New Guinea Jungle? Johanna is simply aghast at the lack of hot showers and ... well ... clothing! She is positive the mission field is most certainly not God's plan for her life, but will that mean letting go of the man she loves? Warm and whimsical, *Monday Morning Faith* will take you on a spiritual journey filled with depth and humor.

Softcover: 0-310-26349-2

Simple Gifts

Lori Copeland

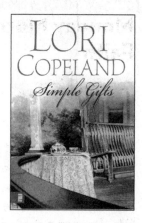

Can anything else go wrong?
Marlene Queens goes home to
Parnass Springs, Missouri, to
put her late Aunt Beth's house
on the market and settle the es-
tate. But once she's back home,
Marlene suddenly finds herself
in over her head. Her Aunt Ingrid grows more demand-
ing by the day. Marlene discovers her childhood sweet-
heart is now the local vet and the town's acting mayor.
And when a group of citizens want to put up a statue
in memory of Marlene's father — the parent who always
embarrassed her as a child — Marlene is unwillingly
swept into a firestorm of controversy.

As one thing leads to another, Marlene sees her
entire life being rearranged before her eyes. Parnass
Springs may never be the same. Marlene fears that the
secret she's kept for years may be revealed. Can God
work a miracle so she can finally have the future she's
longed for?

Softcover: 0-310-26350-6

Pick up a copy today at your favorite bookstore!

Three ways to keep up on your favorite Zondervan books and authors

Sign up for our *Fiction E-Newsletter*. Every month you'll receive sample excerpts from our books, sneak peeks at upcoming books, and chances to win free books autographed by the author.

You can also sign up for our *Breakfast Club*. Every morning in your email, you'll receive a five-minute snippet from a fiction or nonfiction book. A new book will be featured each week, and by the end of the week you will have sampled two to three chapters of the book.

Zondervan *Author Tracker* is the best way to be notified whenever your favorite Zondervan authors write new books, go on tour, or want to tell you about what's happening in their lives.

Visit *www.zondervan.com* and sign up today!

ZONDERVAN®

ZONDERVAN.com/
AUTHORTRACKER
follow your favorite authors